The Jewel
Of
Dahleigh
The Quest

K.J.Port

DEDICATION

I dedicate this book to my mum and dad who have always been there and will always be the two most inspirational people in my life. I also dedicate this to my amazing husband who stays by my side and supports me in whatever I do. To my children who have always been my main inspiration and to my absent friends who have left such and imprint on my life that they live on in every page of this book.

CONTENTS

ACKNOWLEDGMENTS

I would like to thank my family and friends for lots of reasons. Firstly for always encouraging me to follow my dreams and for accepting me for who I am but mostly for having their great personalities to which I could base my characters on, without them there would be no book. A special thank you to my amazing husband Nick for making me believe in my writing again and encouraging me to publish this ten years after I started writing it. To my good friend Farley for his tireless efforts in promoting my book and for teaching me to "Keep on, keeping on!" (KOKO). The biggest thank you has to go to my absent friend Shirley, without her words of wisdom and her strength in her final days, begging me to promise her I would write this book I would not be where I am today and I never would have put pen to paper all those years ago.

The Competition

It was a beautiful Spring Saturday in April, A day like any other. But for two children living in a small village in the South East of Essex something was about to happen that would change their lives forever.

"Ha! Ha! Look at me; I'm the king of the castle." Jordan Chanted. "Look! The little sissy can't even climb the first rock." The young boy laughed and pointed down at the little girl trying to climb onto a rock below.

"Stop it Jordan!" Chloe cried, crossing her arms and stomping her foot.

"Stop it Jordan!" Jordan mimicked. "Chloe you are such a drama queen."

Chloe stomped her foot down once again.

"Kids! Come on its time to go home." Their mum called from a distance.

"O.K. Mum!" They called back in unison. Jordan jumped down

from the rock he was sitting on and raced Chloe back to where their mum was standing waiting for them.

They had all spent the morning exploring the castle ruins close to their home as they did every weekend. As usual they packed a picnic and walked up the hill to the castle ruins where their mum would sit in the same spot and look out at the surrounding countryside. Jordan often teased his mum and said she looked like she was searching the scenery rather than admiring it. But it was the same every weekend; they would explore the ruins and eat a picnic before returning home. Jordan and Chloe loved the weekends. They lived with their mother in a tatty old terraced house in a small village called Hadleigh. Jordan was a typical eleven year old little boy, a bit small for his age with silvery blonde hair and the biggest blue eyes you have ever seen, he always looked immaculate and was very fussy about what he wore and how neat his hair looked. If he didn't have his nose stuck in a book, his eyes were glued to the television. Jordan also loved to tease his little sister Chloe, who was eight and unlike her brother was big for her age and was almost the same size as Jordan. Chloe's mousy brown hair always looked scruffy no matter what her mum tried to do with it, but her big green eyes that where identical to her mums stood out so much you rarely noticed her hair. Chloe loved to sing and dance; in fact it's all she ever seemed to do which really wound Jordan up, much to Chloe's pleasure. Both children absolutely adored their mum, who had always brought them up on her own and though quite poor she always made sure they had what they needed and lavished them with love. At night she made up Enchanting fairytales to tell the children before they went to sleep, then while they were at school she would paint bright colourful pictures of scenes from the story she had told the night before, both Jordan and Chloe thought she was a great

4

artist and could hardly wait to get home from school to see what painting their mum was going to present to them that day.

As soon as Jordan and Chloe had walked through the front door after their morning of exploring the castle ruins, they both threw off their jackets and kicked off their shoes and raced into the lounge to watch the TV.

"I do wish you kids would hang up your coats and put your shoes away, how many times do I have to tell you!" Their mum yelled, who was still making her way through the front door picking up coats and shoes on the way.

"Sorry Mum!" They both called from the lounge.

"Mum look!" Jordan said pointing at the television as his mum walked into the lounge.

"It's that programme you like." He continued. "You know? The one with the big house and all those animals."

"The Estate." His mum said sitting down between the two children, arms spread wide for each child to cuddle in to her.

"Yes that's the one." Jordan replied.

They all cuddled up to watch the programme together. It was filmed at a place called "The Holmes Estate." A huge manor house with great tourist attractions there. It even had a safari park on its grounds. The programme was mainly about the animals in the safari park. This programme had been particularly sad as a beautiful white tiger called Shandy had sadly died and it had lived at The Estate for sixteen years.

"Don't cry mum." Chloe said patting her mum on the hand.

"I know I'm soppy." Their mum laughed and wiping a tear from her cheek. "You know what I'm like with animals and you know how much I would love to go there."

As she said this a familiar face from the programme appeared on the TV screen. An older man, who looked quite eccentric in a bright multi coloured coat.

"Who is that?" Jordan laughed

"That! Is Lord Holmes." His mum replied. "He lives in the big house there."

"Wow!" Both Jordan and Chloe said together.

Lord Holmes began to speak.

"Hello to all my wonderful viewers!" He said in a loud booming voice. "I have a most extraordinary Prize for one lucky family to come and join me here at my estate for a Magical Day out. I will personally guide you around my estate and I might just let you into a few of the secrets here. All you have to do is answer this question." Lord Holmes paused.

"Can I enter mum?" Jordan asked with excitement.

"Shhh!" His mum said. "Let me hear the question."

"The question is." Lord Holmes paused again for a moment then continued. "What are two of my favourite animals here at the safari park?"

"I think it's a lion and a monkey!" Chloe yelled jumping up and down on her seat with excitement.

"No! I think it's a tiger and a Wolf!" Jordan shouted with even more excitement.

"What do you think mum?" Chloe asked.

"I think it's a tapir and a bongo." Their mum said calmly.

"A What!?" Jordan asked with a puzzled look on his face.
"What made you say that?"

"Do you know Jordan. I really don't know?" His mum
answered looking just as puzzled herself that she had given such
a strange answer, after all they weren't every day animals.

"Here you go." She added passing the phone to Jordan after
tapping in the telephone number that was now at the bottom of
the screen. "Why don't you enter?"

Jordan took the telephone and after a few moments pause he
gave the answer that his mother had said, then he gave his
name and their telephone number before hanging up.

"They said they would announce the winner at the end of the
show." Jordan said turning back to the TV to watch the rest of
the programme. When the programme had finished there was
no announcement.

"That isn't fair!" Chloe frowned, crossing her arms and
stomping her foot down as she always did when she wasn't
happy.

"Oh well maybe they'll call the winner instead, you did have to
leave a telephone number after all." Their mum said trying to
ease their disappointment. "You two go and play while I get
dinner ready."

A few hours later they were all seated at the dining table and

7

had just finished eating their dinner when the phone rang. Jordan ran into the lounge to answer it.

"It's for you mum!" He called in a disappointed voice.

"Who is it?" His mum asked. Jordan shrugged his shoulders. She took the phone and after a minute or two of silence she slowly lowered herself onto the sofa with a shocked look on her face, she said the odd "Yes!" or "OK!" to the person at the other end of the telephone. After a few more moments she said thank you then hung up the phone still looking stunned.

"What's the matter mum?" Chloe asked. Who had now joined them in the lounge.

"That was Lord Holmes." Her mum answered then slowly continued. "There was a problem with the programme so he said he wanted to call in person."

"And??" Jordan said with a hint of excitement in his voice.

Both the children were looking wide eyed at their mum, both holding their breath waiting for her reply.

"We won that competition!" Their mum screamed with excitement picking up Chloe and spinning her around then doing the same to Jordan.

Jordan and Chloe could hardly contain their excitement and were now jumping up and down. Their mum, now calm, sat in silence still looking rather stunned that Lord Holmes had actually called in person.

"What did he say mum?" Jordan asked sitting down next to his mum.

"Not much really." His mum answered pulling Chloe towards her and lifting her onto her lap. "He just said that we will be picked up from here tomorrow afternoon and not to worry about accommodation as it had all been arranged. He also said that I'm not to worry about anything and that I should trust him whatever that means." She continued with a frown.

"Tomorrow!" Chloe cried with excitement, jumping down from her mums lap to dance around the lounge.

"Yes tomorrow, so bath and bed." Their mum replied "you first Chloe."

"Ok mum," Chloe said as she sped off upstairs for her bath

"Are you ok mum?" Jordan asked seeing his mum looked a bit down.

"I'm fine my lovely, it's going to be strange to be a guest in such a lovely house." His mum replied giving Jordan a little smile "off you go to bed now."

"Ok, night mum." Jordan said as he stood up and gave his mum a kiss.

"I love you." His mum said softly

"I love you more!" He said back smiling

"I love you most." She replied, blowing him a kiss as he walked off "Catch it."

Jordan put his hand up and caught the kiss she had just blown to him before climbing the stairs to go to bed.

Their mum sighed and looked around the tired looking room,

their house was cold and very run down and indeed much different from the house they would be exploring with Lord Holmes.

That night Jordan and Chloe could hardly sleep they were so excited. Early the next morning Jordan crept into Chloe's room to wake her up.

"I'm so excited." Jordan whispered.

"Me too!" Chloe replied.

"I bet mums more excited than us." Jordan said. "She's always dreamed of going to Holmes Estate. Mum deserves a bit of good luck for a change. We should try and be good for her while we are there."

Chloe nodded in agreement then got out of bed to get dressed. Jordan went into his own room to get dressed. By the time they had both got downstairs their mum was also up and dressed and was now preparing breakfast.

After breakfast they spent the rest of the morning packing some clothes and other things that they needed for their trip. Dead on two o'clock just after they had finished their lunch there was a Beep sound from a car horn outside their house. Jordan flew to open the front door with Chloe close at his heels. Their mum was by now rushing around the house making last minute checks and picking up the bags they had packed that morning. As she walked towards the front door she had her head buried in her handbag checking that she hadn't forgotten her keys.

"Mum. You have got to see this!" Jordan said with sheer amazement in his voice.

Sitting outside their grubby little three bedroom terrace was a huge gleaming white limousine. Jordan and Chloe's mum looked up and froze.

"This is like a fairytale." She said in complete awe before taking Chloe by the hand and leading her towards the magnificent white car stood before them.

"Good afternoon ma'am." The Chauffer said taking off his hat and tucking it under his arm before opening the passenger door for them to climb in.

Jordan and Chloe jumped straight in, they were both chatting excitedly to each other pointing out things that were in the limousine. Their mum was totally speechless and hesitated before climbing in; she smiled nervously at the chauffer then climbed silently into her seat. The chauffer shut the door behind her, loaded their luggage into the boot then climbed into the driving seat. Before starting the engine he lowered the dividing window between the chauffer and the passengers. He turned to face them all resting his chin on his arms.

"Hello Children, I'm Albert your chauffer for the next couple of days." He said smiling at Jordan and Chloe. "Is your mum OK?" He asked laughing and nodding his head towards their mum who was still sat rigid and silent.

Jordan and Chloe laughed.

"Sorry I'm fine." Their mum laughed snapping herself out of her trance like state. "It's just... things like this don't usually happen to us. I mean... It's like a dream!"

Albert smiled sweetly. He was an old man with a large round tummy and silver well groomed hair. He wore an immaculate black suit and had the kindest face you ever did see.

"Well then!" Albert said. "We'll just have to make sure we make it extra special for you all." Before turning back to face forward he focused his attention on the two children and said. "Lord Holmes is particularly eager to meet you two." With that he turned, closed the dividing window and drove away from their house.

The journey there seemed to go really quickly. It took about five hours but with a huge limousine that had a built in TV and a fridge full of snacks and cold drinks, time flew by and before they knew it they were pulling up outside a quaint little bed and breakfast. Albert asked them to wait in the limousine while he took their luggage inside. Moments later he returned and opened the passenger door; slowly they all climbed out and looked around in complete awe at the beautiful old farm house that had now obviously been turned into accommodation for paying guests. Albert looked at their faces and chuckled to himself.

"Here is the key to your room Miss Dean." He said handing her a Key. "It is the family suite on the top floor. Lord Holmes has requested that I tell you to feel free to order anything you desire from room service. I will return at eight A.M. to start your day at The Estate." Albert continued and before climbing back into the limousine he smiled sweetly at them all. "Goodnight ma'am, Goodnight children." Off he went.

"Come on mum, let's go in." Chloe said tugging at her mums' jacket. Slowly they all walked through a magnificent old large wooden door. They were seen up to their room, which was more like an apartment than a room in a large farm house. After the nicest dinner they had ever eaten they all settled down for an early night.

"Can you tell us a story mum?" Chloe asked as she pulled her night dress on over her head and jumped into one of the single beds.

"Yes go on mum. Please." Jordan pleaded as he jumped into the other single bed that was next to Chloe's.

"Tell us the one about the princess and her lost love." Chloe requested.

"Yes I like that one." Jordan added.

"Oh go on then." Their mum replied as she sat down on the end of Chloe's bed.

She told them the story she had told many times about a princess that meets a handsome but peculiar man whilst out walking one day. Every day for a week they met at the same spot and as the week passed they fell hopelessly in love with each other. At the end of the week the man told the princess that he would be unable to meet her the following day but promised he would return the day after, before saying goodbye he gave her his emerald ring as a promise of his return. Two days later the princess went to meet the man but he didn't show up, every day she went back but still he never returned. A year later the princess was forced to marry a very evil prince who was very cruel to her and still to this day the princess returns to the spot searching for her lost love hoping that one day he will return and save her from her cruel husband.

Before their mum had finished the story Jordan and Chloe had fallen asleep. Their mum just sat watching her children sleep for a while, thinking of how happy they looked and how lucky she felt. Before falling asleep herself she gently kissed Jordan and Chloe on the head.

"Goodnight my babies." She whispered. "I hope you'll always remember this."

The Estate

The next morning the farmhouse dining room was just waking up to a quiet stream of guests making their way to breakfast. It was eight fifteen and suddenly the silence was broken by the sound of feet thundering down the stairs.

"Come on kids, we're late!" A voice bellowed from the top of the stairs.

Jordan and Chloe burst out laughing at the fact their mum hadn't even noticed them race past her down the stairs already.

"I can't believe we're late!" Complained Chloe.

"Well it was your fault." Jordan said poking Chloe in the arm.

"No it was not!" Chloe yelled back.

"Stop it now!" Their mum shouted. Pushing open the door that lead out of the bed and breakfast, her head buried in her hand bag checking she had everything. "I won't have you fighting today do you hear me!" As she looked up from her bag she jumped. Albert was stood right in front of her.

"Sorry we're late." She said. "These two are a nightmare to get kick started in the mornings."

She laughed as she nodded her head towards Jordan and Chloe.

Albert chuckled and opened the door of the limousine and they all climbed in.

"Albert?" Chloe said before Albert had a chance to close the door. "What's Lord Holmes like?"

"Mmm! Well the best way I can describe him in one word is magical." Albert answered before smiling and shutting the door.

Minutes later, they were heading down a country lane towards a large forest. Jordan and Chloe were chatting non stop about what they thought the day had in store for them. As they approached the forest they turned and drove down a narrow lane that lead deep into the forest and after a short while the limousine came to a halt and Albert had stepped out and opened the passenger door for them all to get out.

"Welcome to the Holmes Estate." Albert said as he shut the door behind them. "Well the forest part of it anyway."

The forest around them was breathtaking. It was a beautiful sunny day and they stood surrounded by magnificent trees and a sea of spring flowers, it was simply enchanting. Albert led them towards a clearing where a table had been set for them.

"Lord Holmes will be joining you for breakfast ma'am." Albert addressed Jordan and Chloe's mum as he pulled out one of the chairs. "Please be seated."

They all sat down in complete silence and all looked rather nervous. Suddenly a loud booming voice startled them.

"Welcome! Welcome!" Lord Holmes boomed enthusiastically as he walked towards them. He was wearing the same bright multi coloured coat he often wore on the television. He was a man in his fifties, with jet black disheveled hair and a beard with grey patches in it. He did not look like a Lord at all.

He grabbed hold of Jordan's hand and shook it vigorously.

"Ah you must be Jordan." He said. Jordan nodded nervously. "Now this pretty little lady must be young Chloe." He rested his hand on Chloe's cheek before moving on. "You must be the wonderful Miss Dean." He said lifting her hand and kissing it gently.

"Yes I am." Their mum replied blushing slightly. "But please call me Kelly."

Lord Holmes sat down and they all tucked into fresh grapefruit followed by warm croissants.

"So Kelly, I hear you are a lover of Art." Lord Holmes said turning her way.

"Yes." She replied slowly wondering how he knew this.

"Albert!" Lord Holmes Called to Albert who was now sitting on a nearby log. "Take the children for a stroll in the forest for ten minutes or so. Kelly and I would like to talk art for a while, a subject I'm sure these two young children would find an awful bore."

Lord Holmes gave Albert a wink.

"Yes my Lord." Albert replied holding out his hands for each child to hold on to and off they went into the forest leaving Lord Holmes and their mother to talk.

They walked deep into the forest for a while before Jordan looked up and asked. "Albert. How did Lord Holmes know all of our names?

"And he knew mummy liked art!" Chloe added.

"Well I told you he was magical." Albert answered.

"Don't be silly, mum probably said something when she spoke to him on the phone!" Jordan laughed, "Besides, there's no such thing as magic!"

"Yes there is!" Chloe Argued.

"No there isn't!" Jordan yelled back, shoving Chloe to one side. Chloe began to cry.

"Now! Now! Chloe." Albert said kneeling in front of Chloe and wiping a tear from her cheek. "It's OK to believe in magic. Lord Holmes always told me that the more you believe in magic the more chance you have of seeing it. So you just keep on believing."

"Nonsense!" Jordan huffed scuffing a pile of leaves with his shoe.

"Lord Holmes says that this whole place is full of magic, you've just got to believe in it." Albert continued, ignoring Jordan's comment. "He says if you look hard enough you might just catch sight of fairies and such like."

"Fairies!" Chloe Squealed with excitement. "I love fairies; the tooth fairy came to my house last week. Look!" Chloe opened her mouth wide and pointed at a gap in her teeth.

"I told you. There's no such this as Fairies!" Jordan scowled at Chloe.

"Jordan." Albert said now standing and continuing to walk into the forest. "Look around you, I bet if you look hard enough and believed enough you might just catch sight of a healing fairy."

"Now you are being silly!" Scoffed Jordan, he then looked nervously around the forest as if part of him thought it may be true.

"What's a healing fairy?" Chloe asked.

"Well!" Albert began. "Lord Holmes says that each fairy has its own colour. He says that all fairies are born without any colour at all and only tiny little wings and when they get to a certain age they are given a gift and their wings, the gift they are given determines what colour they will be. I believe healing fairies are red."

"Wow!" Chloe cooed. "I thought that fairies would all look the same."

"Not according to Lord Holmes." Albert continued. "He says that he often takes morning strolls in the forest with his good friend Tezla who he claims is a green nature fairy. Apparently the green nature fairies look after the forest and all the animals here but Lord Holmes says they are really hard to spot. They camouflage well in these tree's you see."

"Wow! What about blue fairies, are there blue fairies?" Chloe asked totally amazed by the whole subject.

"Mmm! Let me think." Albert said scratching his head. "Ah yes, music fairies. Lord Holmes says he often hears their sweet music on the breeze when he takes his morning stroll."

"Lord Holmes sounds like a bit of a fruit loop if you ask me!" Jordan mocked

"What other colours are there?" Chloe asked. Trying to ignore the comment Jordan had just made

"Well I do know that yellow fairies are dream fairies, purple ones are flower fairies, pink ones are tooth fairies, oh and orange ones are wish fairies, apparently the orange ones are really fast and hard to catch but if you do happen to catch one it will grant you a wish." Albert answered.

"Wow! Lord Holmes told you all that." Chloe said still in total amazement.

"He didn't have to tell me," Albert replied. "Nothing I see here surprises me anymore, the trouble we had with a leprechaun once it took us ages to chase it away."

"Really! A leprechaun?" Chloe asked. "Why did you chase it away?"

"Well Lord Holmes had apparently been trying to chase it away for years; it was being a right pest." Albert replied. "He finally asked me to help when I spotted it one day, at first I thought I was hallucinating but his Lordship reassured me that I wasn't and told me what the little rascal had been doing."

"What had it been doing?" Chloe asked.

"It kept ripping up the beautiful gardens here." Albert replied.

"And I hear it even killed a few of the smaller animals here."

"It sounds like a nasty leprechaun." Chloe said.

For a moment, Jordan and Chloe just paused and nervously studied the surrounding forest.

"Jeese next you'll be telling me that that tree can really talk and pixies lives in it." Jordan joked pointing at the nearest tree. They all chuckled.

"Lord Holmes would probably say yes to that." Albert laughed. "But then again I think that bright coat he wears might have warped his mind a bit."

Jordan and Chloe burst out laughing.

"Come on let's get you back to your mum so you can start your tour of the estate." Albert said taking the children's hands and leading them back the way they had came.

As they got closer to the clearing where they had left Lord Holmes and their mum talking they could see Lord Holmes standing next to a large land rover that their mum was now seated in.

"Hop aboard children, we're off on safari!" He yelled as they approached the clearing and was now holding open the land rover door.

Jordan and Chloe thanked Albert before running off to jump in.

"I'll see you back at the house!" Albert called after them. "And remember keep believing!" He then winked a knowing wink at Lord Holmes who smiled and nodded back at him before climbing into the land rover himself.

"On with the Tour!" He boomed as they started heading towards the safari park. "There's so much to see, so much to learn, so many adventures to be had and so little time!" He added as he tapped his wristwatch and shook his head.

Jordan and Chloe chuckled to themselves at the very funny Lord Holmes; they knew they were going to like him very much.

"Lord Holmes, is it true that you have fairies here?" Chloe asked. "Albert told us about them when we were in the forest."

"Oh yes my dear." Lord Holmes replied. "They are my good friends."

"Can we see them? Please!" Chloe asked with excitement.

Jordan huffed and rolled his eyes.

"What a load of nonsense!" He sighed under his breath.

"Well we will just have to see about that." Lord Holmes said turning to smile at Jordan.

No one was quite sure whether he was answering Chloe or referring to Jordan's comment about it all being nonsense. Either way no one questioned it.

"First stop, Safari." Lord Holmes boomed as they pulled into a car park near a huge sign that said, "The African Reserve."

"We can jump out here." Lord Holmes continued as he opened his door and hopped out.

Jordan, Chloe and their mum all jumped out and followed Lord Holmes who was now walking towards a small enclosure called Wallaby woods. He led them around and explained all about the wallabies that were in the enclosure resting in groups under a tree. He then continued to walk them around various other enclosures that housed two giant tortoise and some goats. When he got to the giraffe enclosure he stopped.

"We have twelve giraffes now here, three new babies this year." He said pointing towards three small giraffes behind the fence of that enclosure. "Gertrude, Century and Gloria."

"Aw they're so cute." Chloe cooed.

"That there is Ernest." Lord Holmes said now pointing at an ostrich that was in the same enclosure as the giraffes. "There is another ostrich called Honey but she's sitting on her eggs."

"What's a Tapir?" Chloe asked, remembering that was one of the answers to the competition questions

"Follow me and I'll show you." Lord Holmes replied.

They all followed towards yet another enclosure.

"We have three tapirs here." Said Lord Holmes as he peered over the enclosure fence.

They all peered over the fence at three animals that looked rather like brown pigs with fur and long noses. One of them had stripes all over its body.

"Why does that one have stripes?" Jordan asked.

"Because it's still a baby." Lord Holmes replied. "They will disappear when it gets older.

"I like the stripy one." Chloe said. "Do you have a favourite one, as you did say that these were one of your favourite animals?"

"Yes I do. Him!" Lord Holmes said pointing to the biggest of the Tapirs. "That's Bertie; he's rather cheeky he often escapes and comes up to the house to see me."

"Really?" Both Jordan and Chloe said sounding surprised.

"Yes really." Lord Holmes chuckled. "Isn't he a naughty little chap?"

Jordan looked back at the tapir and could have sworn he saw it wink at them.

"Did you see that?" He whispered to Chloe.

"See what?" Chloe replied.

"Oh nothing it was just my imagination." Jordan said shaking his head and rubbing his eyes.

"Right, onto the safari jeep." Lord Holmes boomed enthusiastically as he walked off towards a white jeep that had black stripes painted all over it to make it look like a zebra.

They all jumped into the jeep.

"Windows must be kept shut now." He said as he signalled the driver to proceed.

They drove through various enclosures that housed flamingos, vultures, monkeys that climbed all over the jeep, camels, yaks, Bongos and a deer park where they were allowed to open their windows and feed the deer.

"Windows closed again now, we're entering dangerous

territory." Lord Holmes said seriously as he wound up his window.

Everyone else also wound up their windows before entering the next enclosure. Once the gate to the enclosure was closed behind them they proceeded to look at the tigers, then through another gate to some lions and finally to wolf wood. The whole time Lord Holmes talked about the various animals and of how his father had opened the safari park.

"Well that's the Safari over." He said finally. "I would now like to take you all up to the house."

The jeep drove through a huge archway to reveal a long driveway leading up to the most impressive stately home you have ever seen.

"Welcome to my home." Lord Holmes said smiling proudly.

Jordan, Chloe and their mum were lost for words and sat mouths wide open in total awe of the huge house. The jeep pulled up outside and they all jumped out.

"Good afternoon My Lord." Albert said bowing his head to Lord Holmes as he emerged through the front entrance of the house. "Hello children, Ma'am. Did you enjoy the safari?"

"Yes we did thank you Albert, very much so." Jordan replied for all of them.

"Are we going into that big house now?" Chloe asked looking up at the huge house before her.

"Not yet." Lord Holmes replied. "There is still much to see on the grounds."

"Are you coming with us Albert?" Chloe asked grabbing hold of Albert's hand.

"Is that ok My Lord?" Albert asked.

"Yes of Course it is." Lord Holmes replied.

"Well let's go then." Albert cheered, leading the children around the side of the house. Lord Holmes and their mum followed behind. They were chatting about art again.

The children could not believe the treats that lay just around the corner. A butterfly garden, gift shops, an adventure castle, a train that drove around the grounds of the estate and that's not to mention the various other attractions that they spent hours exploring. They dragged poor Albert this way and that, while Lord Holmes and their mother followed still talking art.

They all sat down for a bite to eat before going on the safari boat that took them down a huge stretch of water that ran along one side of the house. They all hopped aboard the large boat and after minutes of being out in the water the boat was surrounded by sea lions.

"They're hungry," Lord Holmes chuckled as he handed them all some fish to feed to the seals.

"What's that?" Jordan asked pointing to two large mounds in the water.

"Ah they are our two hippos" Lord Holmes replied.

"How cute." The children's mum said.

"Not at all!" Lord Holmes said quite seriously. "In fact they are incredibly dangerous, that's why we have to remain in this large

26

caged boat and try not to disturb them too much, a lesson I wish I had learnt many years ago."

"Why's that?" Chloe asked, "Did one hurt you."

"No, no!" Lord Holmes chuckled. "But it was nearly a different matter. You see, some years back my children kept asking if we could get a boat; finally I gave in and bought a small sailing boat. I thought before taking it out I should test it on my own lake, not my best idea as I was in lots of danger with the hippo's, not knowing at the time how dangerous they were. Luckily, one of the keepers saw me and managed to get my attention and tell me to get off the lake. When he explained why it was so dangerous I was rather pleased that he had been there as things could have gone very wrong."

Jordan laughed as he thought the story was quite funny.

"Jordan don't laugh, it's not funny." Chloe said digging Jordan with her elbow.

Lord Holmes started laughing too.

"It's ok; I find it rather funny myself!" He said.

They continued with their boat ride around the lake, Jordan and Chloe could not stop chatting about things they kept spotting along the way. Once they had done a complete circle of the whole lake they stopped back at the spot they had first boarded the boat.

"I think it's time I took you into the house." Lord Holmes said as they all climbed off the safari boat.

"I have to go now." Albert said. "But I'm sure I will see you later."

Albert winked at Lord Holmes before disappearing through one of the gardens. Lord Holmes led them all back to the grand entrance of the house.

"Shall we madam?" He said holding out his arm for the children's mum to hold onto before proceeding up the stone stairs into the house.

"I'll take you to the public side of the house first." He said as he entered the first long grand corridor. "I try keeping this part of the house preserved in its former glory although some of the rooms are from different time periods."

They all walked with Lord Holmes in the preserved half of the building, with furniture, paintings and other artefacts that must have been hundreds of years old. Lord Holmes talked about the history of each room as they made their way around the house. It was so fascinating. Jordan and Chloe loved looking at all the old objects and listening to all the weird and wonderful things Lord Holmes had to say about each room, the Holmes family and their history at the estate.

"Would you like to see my paintings, my private apartments in the west wing?" Lord Holmes asked as he completed his tour of that part of the house.

"Yes please!" The children's mum replied enthusiastically before the children had a chance to.

He led them to the west wing and into the first room.

"This is the drawing room." He said as they all entered the room. "I call this evolution."

They all looked at the colourful paintings Lord Holmes had painted that covered the room. All of the art looked almost three-dimensional. The children's mum looked like she was in heaven admiring the detail of every painting.

Jordan and Chloe were now stroking a brown Labrador that was sitting in the room.

"Ah! That is Toby." Lord Holmes said stroking the dog.

"He is beautiful." The children's mum said kneeling down and stroking Toby.

"Isn't he?" Lord Holmes replied. "It was love at first sight. Both his parents were golden Labradors as was all his brothers and sisters he was the only brown one so I just had to have him. Do you believe in love at first sight Kelly?"

"Yes, I um... I..." She stammered as she fiddled with a ring on her finger. This question had obviously caught her by surprise.

Lord Holmes simply smiled knowingly at her and continued with his tour.

"Come on Toby!" He called as they left the drawing room.

Toby jumped up and walked beside Chloe.

"He likes you." Lord Holmes said as they entered the next room.

He led them in and out of various rooms showing them all the Paintings he had done.

"Now this room I wanted to leave till last. The Nursery!" Lord Holmes said as he stopped outside a door. "Kelly my dear you

K.J.Port

are going to love this."

He opened the door and led them into the room.

"These are my fantasy paintings." Lord Holmes said.

"Mum it's like the pictures you do about our stories." Chloe said looking up at the walls that were covered with the most breath taking fantasy pictures you have ever seen, with all kinds of mythical creatures and fairy-tale scenes in them

"Only a lot bigger." Jordan added.

They all chuckled.

"Mine are terrible compared to this." Their mum replied. "Your work is so inspiring Lord Holmes."

"Thank you Kelly." He replied.

"I w…." Lord Holmes began before he was interrupted by Toby barking.

"What is it?" He said patting Toby on the head to try to calm him down.

"It's Bertie!" Chloe squealed pointing under a table to what Toby had been barking at.

"Bertie you naughty little tapir, have you escaped again?" Lord Holmes laughed and winked at the Tapir.

Jordan, Chloe and their mum all laughed at the site of seeing a wild animal in a huge manor house.

"I wish this was my bedroom." Chloe said dreamily. "It's magical."

"Everything's magical to you." Jordan snapped. "It's so sissy!"

"Stop it!" Chloe whined stomping her foot down.

Their mum threw them both a look that told them this was no way to be behaving in front of a Lord.

"You don't believe in magic Jordan?" Lord Holmes asked.

"No sir." Jordan replied. "Magic is for sissies!"

"Mmm, that won't do at all." Lord Holmes said frowning. "I believe in magic, does that make me, a sissy as you call it?"

"Uh no sir... I ..." Jordan stammered and turned bright red with embarrassment.

Toby started to bark again but this time he appeared to be barking at the wall.

"There, there Toby." Chloe said gently stroking him to calm him down; Toby instantly stopped barking but still stared at the wall.

Bertie had now emerged from under the table and was sitting at Lord Holmes feet.

"Magic is the essence of The Holmes Estate" Lord Holmes continued. "It's even within these walls, every object, every animal, every stone and every mural holds its own magic. It's a place where mankind and the animal kingdom dwell as one and that of fantasy and myth."

"Now I think he really is mad." Jordan whispered to Chloe.

Chloe put her hand to her mouth to stifle a little chuckle.

Jordan looked up to study the mural again.

"I still don't believe in magic." He said stubbornly.

"I bet I can make you believe in magic." Lord Holmes said smiling at Jordan.

"Yeah right." Jordan said under his breath.

"Shall we press on?" Lord Holmes said now changing the subject.

As Jordan turned to leave the room, he could have sworn that he saw one of the butterflies on a painting flutter its wings.

"Hold on d...d...did that b...b...butterfly just move?" He stammered.

Lord Holmes winked and looked at the painting.

Jordan looked back at the butterfly that was now motionless. He then stepped forward to study it closer. As he stepped forward, he felt himself being drawn to it, closer and closer until his nose was almost touching it. He felt like his whole body was being pulled toward the butterfly and he had no control over it. as his nose touched the painting he felt like his face was being sucked into it, his heart started to beat fast, something wasn't right, why was he being drawn to the painting like that? He started to panic and thrust out an arm and grabbed Chloe to try to pull himself back but he kept being sucked in further and further now pulling Chloe with him. Suddenly they both disappeared.

"Of you go Bertie?" Lord Holmes said ushering the Tapir towards the mural.

Bertie ran towards the wall, leapt into the mural and disappeared.

"Don't worry I told you before they'll be fine." Lord Holmes said to the children's mother who was now staring at the spot her children had just disappeared into looking rather worried. "Bertie will keep them safe and keep us informed of their progress."

"Are you sure?" She replied with a scared look on her face. "I have nothing without them, they're my whole life."

"I give you my word." Lord Holmes replied.

"How about a nice glass of wine and a game of chess my dear?" He asked before taking her arm and leading her out of the nursery.

Dahleigh

"Beau! Where are you?" A beautiful white unicorn bellowed as she charged along a grand corridor in a palace towards two huge golden doors at the far end. "Beau, please we're going to be late!" The unicorn said this time in a much softer tone as she walked through the golden doors that lead into a grand bedroom. The bedroom had a gigantic bay window with pretty pink drapes at one end and a huge silver four poster bed at the other.

The unicorn looked around the room for a second, and then out of the corner of her eye she saw one of the large drapes at the window twitch. The Unicorn smiled sneakily to herself.

"Hmm! Where can she be?" The unicorn said out loud. "I wonder! Well I suppose I better go and tell the King that his daughter will not be attending her own ceremony."

"No! Stop! Please don't." Came a voice from behind the drape. The Unicorn Chuckled.

"Well we can't get you ready from behind there." The unicorn said. "Are you going to come out?"

"No!" The voice behind the drape said stubbornly.

The unicorn walked towards the huge bay window and looked out of it.

"Beau, come on today's your big day." She said still focusing her attention out of the window. "It's your twelfth birthday, we have prepared for this since the day you were born and I became your chaperon. Besides I've had to listen to you go on for years and years about this colour you want to be or that colour you want to be, well today you finally find out. I know you must be nervous but..."

"It's not that." The voice interrupted from behind the drape. "Well look at me!"

A little fairy emerged from behind the drape, it was covered with paint all the colours of the rainbow. Her head held low in a sulk. The unicorn started to laugh and the little fairy jumped back behind the drapes.

"I was only trying on the colours to see what one suited me best!" The little fairy huffed before tucking her head behind the drape too.

The unicorn stopped laughing and looked back out of the window.

"Look at all those fairies down there!" She said now focusing out the window to a courtyard below that was now filling up with fairies of all different colours. "They're all here in honour of you Beau! You are the princess after all."

The little fairy stepped out from behind the drape and stood next to the unicorn. They watched the fairies below making their way to the courtyard which was already full. Every now and then one shot straight past the window rushing to get a seat in the courtyard.

"I've been here over a hundred years and still it takes my breath away." The unicorn said now focusing beyond the courtyard full to the brim with fairies to the breathtaking view beyond the palace. Fields of purple grass stretched out just past the palace walls with the most exotic flowers you have ever seen. Just beyond the fields was a forest that bore trees of many different colours that from where they was standing looked like multi coloured balls of cotton candy. In the distance you could just catch the glow from the silvery lake on the horizon that stretched out in front of a pink snowcapped mountain.

"Dahleigh is a big world and here we are in one small corner of it." The unicorn said now looking at the little fairy still covered in paint.

"When you get your wings Dahleigh will be yours to explore. There is so much it has to offer. Creatures you have only dreamed about or heard me talk about. Whatever happens today it is your destiny, it always was your destiny since the day you were born. My! It only seems like yesterday I first set eyes on the most precious little fairy I had ever seen. Even then I could tell great things were in store for you and although you lay there so tiny, grey and transparent I knew that your personality and nature would outshine any colour. Today you will be given a gift and I know that whatever that gift is you'll embrace it with all your heart."

Beau the little fairy threw her arms around the unicorns' neck.

"I love you so much Nee." She said.

A tear glimmered in Nee's eye. For today was also to be the last day she would act as Beau's chaperon. They had grown extremely close as you would expect. Nee had chaperoned ten generations of Beau's family but had grown particularly fond of Beau.

Beau could sense what Nee was thinking.

"I'm going to miss you." She said. "How am I going to cope without you?"

"You know I'll always be here if you need me." Nee said choking back her tears. "You were my best assignment yet, I know that great things are in store for you Beau and I know that whatever challenge comes your way you'll be able to deal with it without my help."

Beau wiped away the tear now trickling down Nee's cheek then kissed Nee on the nose.

"Come on let's get you cleaned up!" Nee said, trying to ease the emotional tension between them. "We can't be having the princess of Dahleigh turning up looking like a mixed up rainbow can we!?"

They both remained silent while Beau cleaned off all the paint and prepared herself for her birthday banquette. Beau sat down at her dressing room table and took one last look at herself in the mirror.

"I look so dull!" She huffed, frowning at her grey transparent reflection. Then she turned and fluttered two tiny grey wings upon her back. "As for these silly little wings boy I can't wait to get bigger ones."

"Well it's not for much longer." Nee chuckled. She placed the finishing touch on Beau's head. A silver crown with crystals the shape and colour of little daisy's all entwined to look like a daisy chain.

"I wonder how Chi's getting on." Beau said.

Chi was Beau's very best friend who also shared the same birthday as her, so today he would also be receiving his colour and wings. They were extremely close more like brother and sister than best friends. Chi's mother had died when he was a tiny baby and his father was often away travelling various forests around Dahleigh so he often lived at the palace while his father was away. Chi said his father was searching Dahleigh for hidden portholes to other worlds but Beau knew his father was a green nature fairy who travelled Dahleigh looking after the forests and animals, Beau also knew that Chi loved making up stories.

"I hope his dad's there." Beau continued. "And I hope he does end up a blue fairly like his mum was."

"If only she were still alive." Nee said choking back a tear. "She would have loved this. Do you know his mum and your mum were just like you and him, thick as thieves."

Nee chuckled as she thought back to when Beau and Chi's mothers had received their colour and wings.

"Chi is so much like his mother." Nee continued now looking sombre again.

"How did his mum die?" Beau asked. "He doesn't know and

his dad won't talk about it."

"Yes I wonder if Chi is ready yet." Nee said, obviously changing the subject and avoiding the question. "I'm sure he's probably ready and raring to go! But I'm sure the princess is delaying proceedings by being so late!"

Beau looked up at the clock and starting to panic.

"Your father will be turning grey if we don't hurry up!" Nee added as she ushered Beau to get a move on.

Beau jumped up and they both rushed out of the golden doors, down the grand staircase and along a corridor towards the courtyard.

Beau's heart was thumping hard and suddenly she felt very nervous. She looked at the huge green door at the end of the corridor that led out to the courtyard and swallowed hard. When they got to the door they stopped. She could hear the crowd of fairies on the other side of the door all cheering and chanting.

"Pull yourself together!" Beau said to herself. Her heart now feeling like it was going to jump out of her chest.

"I am so proud of you Beau." Nee said, looking affectionately at Beau.

Beau smiled nervously back at Nee before they both turned to face the door ready to make their entrance.

In the courtyard, the crowd of fairies fell silent as a horn began to sound. All their eyes were focused upon a huge archway of flowers where beneath stood a little plump blue fairy holding a trumpet shaped flower to his lips. He lowered the flower and puffed out his chest before bellowing.

"All rise and be standing for King Oberon, Queen Peri and their son and heir Prince Avery!"

The crowd of fairies stood to attention and then burst into applause as three fairies entered the courtyard and sat on three wonderful thrones made from orchids that had been placed beneath the floral arch at one end of the courtyard.

King Oberon was Beau's adoring father and being the King was golden in colour as was his wife Queen Peri. Avery was Beau's older Brother and heir to the throne and being the heir he was silver.

King Oberon stood to address the crowd of fairies stood before him; they all fell silent and waited for him to speak.

"Welcome!" He said smiling. "Today is a truly momentous day for us all. A day that my heart and that of my Queen is so full of pride."

King Oberon turned to face the most beautiful golden fairy you have ever seen. Queen Peri smiled at her husband sweetly.

"My daughter has finally reached her twelfth birthday, so today we hold a banquette in honour of her receiving her colour and wings and with these I'm sure Dahleigh holds great adventures for her."

Dahleigh held colouring ceremonies almost every day that the king and queen would attend, but usually it would be a small affair with just the fairy that is receiving their colour and their families. However today being the princesses' birthday and colouring day every fairy for miles had turned up to join in with the celebration.

King Oberon paced backwards and forwards for a while deep in thought before stopping and turning to nervously face Queen Peri who nodded as if to prompt him to continue.

"Right!" He said shaking the thoughts from his head. "It is time for The Ceremony of Colours, but before we begin it is with my deepest affection and proudest pleasure I present to you my beautiful daughter Princess Beau!"

All eyes turned to face a huge green door at the opposite end of the courtyard. The door opened slowly and in walked Nee followed by a very nervous Beau, who always hated big public displays. She could feel thousands of eyes staring at her so she tried to duck behind Nee.

"Remember head up, shoulders back and please smile!" Whispered Nee.

Beau straightened her back, took a deep breath and nervously smiled before proceeding to walk down the long floral aisle towards her father.

The courtyard burst into a chorus of cheers and applause as Beau made her way to go and stand next to her father. Beau nodded at the on looking crowd before turning to take her seat in a throne next to her mother, who was smiling proudly at her.

"Thank you." King Oberon said, addressing the crowd once more. "Now I'm sure my daughter is eager to get on with her party, but before we do we need to proceed with the usual Ceremony of Colours."

King Oberon paused as four grey transparent fairies entered the courtyard through the green door and made their way down the aisle. They all knelt before King Oberon and bowed their heads.

"How lucky you are to share a birthday with my beloved daughter." King Oberon said.

As he did, one of the fairies looked up at Beau and smiled. Beau smiled back.

"Good luck Chi." She mimed at the little fairy still knelt before her father.

"Thank you, and you." Chi mimed back, before standing to face the crowd of fairies, as did the other three fairies that had been kneeling before King Oberon.

"Let the Ceremony begin!" King Oberon boomed. He then nodded his head towards an orchestra of blue fairies. The orchestra picked up their instruments and began to play.

King Oberon looked up at the sky and muttered something under his breath before pointing his finger straight upwards. Dark clouds started forming in the sky above them and it began to rain softly. He then muttered something else as he started waving his finger around. Two clouds separated to reveal a blazing hot sunshine, seconds later a rainbow burst from the sky, the end of it landing just before King Oberon's' feet. The crowd of fairies burst into a sea of applause, and then turned their eyes to the four grey fairies stood beneath the floral arch. All four fairies and Beau suddenly looked very nervous.

"Chi, please step forward." King Oberon requested.

Chi stepped forward and approached King Oberon.

"Ah my dear Chi, you're more like a son to me." The King continued as he affectionately patted Chi on the head. "I couldn't be prouder, both you and my very own Beau receiving your colour on the very same day. I know your mother would have been so proud."

"Thank you so much for looking after me." Chi said, forgetting where he was he threw his arms around King Oberon and hugged him tightly. King Oberon laughed which reminded Chi there was a whole crowd of fairies watching him. He let go of the king and looked quite embarrassed.

"Go on, what are you waiting for? Off you go." King Oberon said nodding his head towards the rainbow.

Chi swallowed hard and turned to Search the crowd for his father. He then turned and looked disappointingly at Beau.

"I'm sure he is there." Beau mimed to try to reassure her best friend. She then nodded her head to prompt him to go on. The little grey fairy turned back to face the rainbow, he closed his eyes before stepping into it. As he emerged through the other side, his body started turning blue and on his back formed two magnificent wings.

"Good!" Beau said to herself. "He wanted to be a music fairy, just like his mum was."

Chi nervously looked down at his body, and then looked up at Beau a smile beaming from ear to ear. He then fluttered his wings and flew to where he was now to be seated amongst the crowd. As he flew, a trail of blue fairy dust scattered behind him.

King Oberon called the next fairy, who went through the rainbow and emerged the other side orange, the next one was purple and the last one was pink.

"Mum I'm scared." Beau whispered to the Queen.

"You're such a sissy!" Prince Avery teased. "What are you worried about, what's the worst that could happen? The rainbow will realise what a sissy you are and turn you multi coloured."

Nee, who was standing nearby laughed to herself as she pictured the paint covered Beau that had stood before her earlier that day.

"At least I'll be able to DO! Magic." Beau mocked. "And don't call me a sissy."

Queen Peri gave Avery a look that told him now was not the time to be teasing. Avery slouched into his throne.

"Right, last but by all means not least it is my daughters turn to step through the rainbow." King Oberon said. He took Beau by the hand as she rose from her throne; she gave her mother a kiss before hugging and kissing her father.

"We are so very proud of you." Queen Peri said. Her eyes welled up with tears. "Look at you all grown up."

King Oberon choked back a tear as he stood aside for his daughter to step into the rainbow. Beau looked at Chi who smiled at her. She then focused on a fairy stood beside Chi. One fairy was holding a tiny grey baby in her arms. She thought of the journey that tiny fairy had ahead of it, the frustrations of being so dull and the anticipation of what colour it's going to be

44

when it too turns twelve. Beau then turned to look at her beloved Nee. Nee nodded at Beau and smiled.

"Go ahead." She prompted.

Beau took a deep breath and closed her eyes.

"This is it!" She thought to herself. She just stood holding her breath with her eyes shut tight for a while before stepping forward into the rainbow.

For a while everything sounded muffled, she could almost feel the particles of the rainbow brush her face like dust blowing in the wind and as she emerged through the other side she heard the crowd and the Music that the Orchestra had still been playing, suddenly fall silent. She daren't open her eyes.

"Maybe I'm still in the rainbow." She thought to herself, but then she heard Chi gasp from the crowd. Slowly she opened her eyes and looked down.

Her body was still grey and transparent and her wings still tiny. Beau turned to King Oberon for an answer but he looked just as stunned, she then turned to her mother who also looked stunned. Beau's head started spinning; she looked anxiously at the crowd of fairies whose eyes were fixed in stunned silence on her. She turned to Nee.

"What's wrong with me?" She asked, tears now streaming down her cheeks. "Why am I still grey like this?"

The Keeper of Dahleigh

Beau buried her head in her hand and sobbed. Nee went to comfort her, as she did the rainbow disappeared back into the sky and the grey clouds disintegrated away leaving the sun beating down on them all.

"I don't understand?" King Oberon said looking completely puzzled.

Everyone else remained silent.

Queen Peri joined Nee in comforting her daughter.

No one knew what to do or what to say.

Suddenly the silence was broken by a thundering sound getting louder and louder. All the fairies huddled together nervously; Beau snuggled in close to Nee and Queen Peri. A high mountain of rocks to the side of them started to tremble, then from over the top of them burst a spray of water forming a magnificent waterfall. The crowd of fairies gasped.

"What's going on?" Beau whispered to Nee.

"Shiranne is coming." Nee answered, not taking her eyes off the waterfall

"Who's coming?" Beau asked, completely puzzled.

"Shh! Just watch." Nee said.

Through the waterfall emerged a beautiful white tiger, upon its back sat a truly stunning white fairy. The tiger walked towards Beau, who was now clinging onto Nee for dear life.

"Shiranne! Good to see you again." King Oberon said, smiling at the stunning white fairy.

"It's good to see you too King Oberon." Shiranne replied. "It's been a long time. Twelve years in fact."

"You've told me stories about her." Beau said to Nee under her breath.

Nee simply nodded in response.

"Ah! My sweet little Beau." Shiranne said, now looking towards the little grey fairy trying to hide behind Nee. Nee moved leaving Beau totally exposed.

"You know my name." Beau said in amazement.

"Yes, of course I do my dear." Shiranne replied. "I know the names of every fairy here for I am Shiranne, the keeper of Dahleigh."

"But I thought it was only a story, a legend, I didn't realise you were actually real!" Beau said, looking at the beautiful white fairy in complete awe.

"Oh! I am very real." Shiranne laughed. "How time flies, last time I saw you it was the day you was born."

"I remember," Queen Peri said. "You said that you would return on Beau's twelfth birthday, to be honest it had completely slipped my mind."

"Well it has been twelve years." Shiranne replied. "And here I am."

"So you know why I'm still like this then." Beau said looking down at her still grey transparent body.

"Indeed I do." Shiranne said. She then turned to face the crowd. "Every fairy here has a destiny, a gift they will use, just like your little friend Chi down there.

Chi, although now being blue had turned scarlet red with embarrassment.

"His gift is to bring music and life to even the darkest of places." Shiranne continued. "Your destiny however is not to be quite as simple. In time you will realise that you are no ordinary fairy."

"I don't understand." Beau said.

"You will." Shiranne said. She smiled knowingly to herself.

Beau now looked even more puzzled as did every other fairy in the courtyard.

"King Oberon, may we have a word in private?" Shiranne said, now facing the king. "And you Queen Peri, if you don't mind?"

"Certainly." King Oberon replied.

He led Shiranne, who was still sat upon the great white tiger and Queen Peri towards the huge green door. The crowd of fairies watched as they left the courtyard. When they had disappeared from sight the crowd turned to face Beau, for a while they remained silent before gradually breaking into muffled whispers. Every now and then one would point at Beau.

"Nee, what's going on?" Beau asked.

"Wait and see." Nee replied, she smiled down at Beau.

"Beau, I'm sorry for what I said before." Prince Avery said, now joining them from his throne. He looked as if what he had said about the rainbow had somewhat come true.

"It's not your fault." Beau said as she smiled up at her brother.

"Nee, honestly what is going on?" Avery asked.

"I can't say." Nee answered.

"So you do know!" Beau said. She looked anxiously into Nee's eyes.

Nee could not look Beau in the eye so she turned away.

"Nee please tell me." Beau continued.

Chi had now rushed over to be with his best friend.

"You look lovely." Beau said admiring her friends' new blue appearance.

Chi bowed his head, he did not really know what to say, his own appearance didn't seem to matter now, so he just threw his arms around Beau and gave her a huge hug.

"I'm glad you're blue just like your mum was." Beau continued trying to hold back her tears. She was so pleased that her friend had got his wish but felt so frightened and confused herself.

Chi stood back and smiled sweetly at Beau also trying hard to hold back his own tears for his best friend. He dare not mention that he still hadn't spotted his father in the crowd.

Suddenly they were interrupted by King Oberon bursting through the green door followed by Queen Peri and the tiger that was carrying Shiranne on its back. The crowd fell silent once more as the king made his way down the aisle towards his daughter. Chi quickly rushed back to stand in the crowd of fairies. Shiranne once again approached Beau.

"I have explained the situation to your parents." She said. "And they have agreed to accept your quest. That is of course if you also agree."

"Quest! What do you mean quest?" Beau asked.

"I told you Beau, you are no ordinary fairy." Shiranne replied. "And because of this you need to go on a quest to earn your colour."

"What do I have to do?" Beau asked.

"You have to find The Jewel of Dahleigh." Shiranne replied.

"I have to find the what!?" Beau said with a tone of both panic and confusion.

"The Jewel of Dahleigh." Shiranne repeated.

"What is The Jewel of Dahleigh?" Avery asked before Beau had a chance to again.

"Beau will know when she finds it." Shiranne said as she smiled down at Beau.

"Now I'm totally confused." Beau sighed.

"Don't worry." Shiranne said. "I will point you in the right direction and as I said you will know when you find it."

"Shiranne has agreed to let someone go with you." King Oberon said.

"Ooh me! Pick me! Please!" Chi's little voice shouted excitingly from the crowd.

"I'm sorry my dear little Chi." King Oberon said. "You have only just received your gift so therefore we feel you're not ready for such a quest."

Both Chi and Beau looked utterly disappointed. Beau then turned to look at Nee.

"I'm sorry, I'm not allowed." Nee said, reading Beau's thoughts.

"We have already decided that Avery should go." King Oberon announced.

"Oh no dad. Please don't make me go." Avery grumbled.

"Not him dad! Anyone but him." Beau whined at the same time.

"Enough!" King Oberon shouted.

"But he can't even do…" Beau started.

"Avery, please." Queen Peri pleaded, interrupting her daughter and giving her a look that told her to be quiet. "She is your sister and I can't trust anybody else to look after her."

Avery totally adored his mother and found it hard to say no.

"If I must." He said reluctantly.

Beau opened her mouth to argue but knew it wouldn't change their minds so she decided not to say anything.

"Right, it is decided then." King Oberon boomed. "Prince Avery will be your chaperon."

"Right it's time I set you on your way." Shiranne said. "When you leave the palace go through the forest towards the silvery lake, go across the lake and over the pink snow-capped mountain that's on the other side. Then you need to walk across a field until you reach a maze, when you do you'll know that you are half way there."

"And then what?" Avery asked.

"Beau will know what to do." Shiranne replied. "All she has to do is follow her heart."

Nobody dare ask anything else, especially Beau she was confused enough.

"Best you get going before night falls." Queen Peri said as she kissed and hugged both of her children. "Please look after each other."

"We will." They answered in unison.

"Good luck." Nee said, now stepping forward to kiss Beau on the head. She then turned and bowed to Prince Avery.

"Show me what a great king you will be someday, make me proud." King Oberon said hugging his son tightly and patting him on the back. "You look after my princess."

"Don't worry dad, I will." Prince Avery replied, although looking rather nervous.

Beau gave her brother a knowing look and sniggered under her breath.

"Ah and my little princess." King Oberon said as he moved along to hug his daughter. "Not so little anymore. Please be careful and try and do what your brother asks."

"I'll try." Beau replied, squeezing her dad tighter. "I am a bit scared though."

"Don't be scared my beautiful Beau." King Oberon said touching his daughter softly on the cheek. "Your mother and I would never agree to this if we didn't feel like you was ready for it. I have always admired your strength and courage, since the day you was born it shone through above every other fine quality you have. I think... no I know that you can do this."

"Thanks dad." Beau said looking adoringly at her father.

"Before you go, there's one more thing." Shiranne said. The tiger she was sat upon walked towards the waterfall. "There will be somebody else accompanying you on your quest. They should be here any second now."

As she said this two figures emerged through the waterfall.

"What are they?" Beau asked, curling her nose up at the two strange creatures that had just emerged through the waterfall.

"They're humans." Shiranne replied.

"Great, something else I didn't think actually existed." Beau said, frowning to herself.

Nee gave a little chuckle.

Suddenly Beau felt quite scared of the two strange looking creatures stood in front of the waterfall.

"Now I am scared." She said, grabbing Avery by the hand.

"Don't be such a sissy!" He teased as he tried to pull his hand away.

Meanwhile Jordan and Chloe, who had just been sucked into a painting and out of a waterfall, stood frozen with fear. Jordan's mouth was gaped wide open in disbelief at the sight of the sea of fairies stood before them.

"What just happened?" He whispered to Chloe with a shaky voice.

"Now do you believe in magic?" Chloe replied in a whisper.

Jordan slowly nodded his head, his mouth still wide open in amazement.

"Jordan I'm scared!" Chloe said grabbing Jordan's hand.

"Don't be such a sissy!" He said in a nervous voice as he snatched his hand away.

Shiranne climbed down from the white tigers back and slowly

walked towards Jordan and Chloe, as she did diamonds and white butterflies trailed from her dress and wings.

"Don't be frightened children." She said, smiling at them both.

"Wow! You're beautiful." Chloe cooed, no longer feeling scared at all.

Jordan remained frozen with fear, his mouth still wide open.

"Thank you Chloe." Shiranne replied, smiling sweetly at Chloe.

"You know my name!" Chloe gasped.

"Indeed I do, and this is Jordan." Shiranne said now looking at the stunned Jordan.

Chloe elbowed her brother to snap him out of his trance like state.

"I've been expecting you both." Shiranne continued.

"Have you really." Jordan said in a dreamy voice.

"Don't mind him." Chloe laughed. "He didn't believe in magic five minutes ago so I think it's come as a bit of a shock."

Shiranne laughed and held out her hand for Chloe to hold. Chloe hesitated before she nervously took Shirannes hand.

"Come, there's someone I'd like you to meet." Shiranne said as she led Chloe, followed by Jordan towards King Oberon and his family.

"This is King Oberon." Shiranne continued. "And this is his lovely wife Queen Peri and their children Prince Avery and Princess Beau."

They all nervously said hello to each other.

"Lord Holmes has sent you to help Princess Beau on her quest." Shiranne went on. "I'm afraid Princess Beau and Prince Avery will have to fill you in on the details on the way. It's getting late and you must all get going."

"But we can't!" Jordan stammered nervously. "Our mum must be so worried about us. I mean one minute we were all standing in a room looking at a picture and the next thing we're here, our mum must be going mad with worry. No this can't be real I'm dreaming and I'm going to wake up any minute"

Jordan quickly rubbed his eyes in a panic as if he were trying to wake himself up from a dream.

"This is no dream." Chloe Said pinching her brother to prove that he was awake and it was all real.

"Ouch that hurt!" He shouted rubbing his arm.

"Look! What's that?" Chi interrupted from the crowd of fairies. He was pointing at the waterfall.

Everyone in the whole courtyard turned to look at what he was pointing too.

A small figure emerged through the waterfall and hurried towards the children.

"Bertie!" Chloe squealed, looking at the tapir that had just emerged through the waterfall.

"Sorry I'm late." Bertie said. "I took the wrong waterfall."

"You can talk!" Jordan said his mouth once again wide open in amazement. "Now I know I am dreaming!"

"Of course I can talk." Replied Bertie. "I'm in Dahleigh now."

"Dahleigh!" Both the children said in unison.

"We're actually inside the painting." Chloe said, her mouth was now also gaped wide open.

"Yes Dahleigh is Lord Holmes Painting." Bertie said as he walked over to join them. "Oh and by the way your mother is fine, Lord Holmes is looking after her, they have sent me to keep an eye on you."

"Hello Bertie, it's so good to see you again." Shiranne said walking over to give the little tapir a gentle stroke on the head. "I wondered if you were coming, Lord Holmes said to expect you."

"It's good to see you too." Bertie replied looking up in admiration at Shiranne. "Still as stunning as ever I see."

Shiranne looked down at Bertie and gave him a sweet smile followed by another stroke on the head.

"You know each other?" Chloe said looking rather puzzled.

"Of course we do." Bertie replied. "Lord Holmes did kind of create Dahleigh after all."

"How?... Why...? What do you mean?" Jordan stammered still trying to take in all that had happened.

"I'll explain on the way." Bertie said still smiling up at Shiranne, he looked at her in complete awe. She was so beautiful.

"Sorry to interrupt." Shiranne said. "But it's time for you all to go."

Avery and Beau said their final farewell to their friends and family.

"Good luck!" Shiranne said as she walked back towards the waterfall.

"Come on Shandy." She beckoned to the tiger before they both disappeared into the waterfall, which then disappeared back over the mountain of rocks from where it had emerged.

With that, the four children and the Tapir all set off together in silence on their journey to help Beau find "The Jewel of Dahleigh."

Before they disappeared through the gates that lead out of the palace Beau turned to wave at Chi, she hated that she had to leave him behind; they had grown up together and were inseparable. They had planned all the adventures they would have when they had received they're colour and wings and now Beau had to do it without him.

Chi waved sadly back as the group disappeared from sight.

The Quest begins

Two fairies, two children and a Tapir walked in silence, away from the palace towards a forest in the distance. Occasionally one would glance nervously to another then quickly look away so not to make eye contact.

"Ah! I can't bare it anymore." Bertie yelled, finally breaking the silence. "Somebody, please say something."

"So are you a human too?" Beau asked looking down at the little Tapir.

"Yes I am." Bertie answered, not paying any attention to his answer.

"No you're not, you're an animal." Chloe laughed.

"A Tapir, to be precise." Jordan added.

"That's what I meant!" Bertie grumbled. "I wasn't listening."

"Yeah he's an animal you silly sissy." Avery teased Beau. "Didn't you know that?"

"Stop calling me that!" Beau whined, she crossed her arms and stomped her foot down. "And you didn't know what it was either."

Jordan looked at Avery and laughed.

"Sisters, who'll have them." He said.

"There, there Beau." Chloe said comforting Beau. "My brother calls me that all the time too, but I think he's just a big stupid head!"

Beau laughed and with that, the ice was broken.

"So what's this quest all about?" Jordan asked as they continued walking towards the forest.

"Well its Beau's quest really." Avery replied. "It's her twelfth birthday you see and today she was meant to receive her colour and wings."

"Wow what Albert said in the forest was really true." Chloe interrupted. "By the way, Happy Birthday Beau."

"Thanks." Beau replied smiling sweetly at Chloe.

"Don't interrupt, Chloe!" Jordan moaned at his sister. "Sorry Avery, do carry on."

Chloe poked her tongue out at Jordan and turned back to listen to Avery.

"Well the bottom line is..." Avery continued. "It didn't work. She stepped into the rainbow that colour and was meant to come out another."

"Shiranne, that stunning white fairy back there came and said I had to go on a quest." Beau interrupted.

"Yeah, she said it's because Beau isn't normal but I always knew that anyway." Avery teased.

Jordan was the only one that laughed at the backhanded comment.

"Stop teasing me!" Beau whined

"Ignore them." Chloe said rolling her eyes at Jordan and Avery. "So tell me Beau, what do you have to do on this quest?"

"I've got to find The Jewel of Dahleigh." Beau replied.

"What's The Jewel of Dahleigh?" Jordan asked.

"That's just it!" Avery said before Beau had a chance to answer for herself. "We don't know! Shiranne just said Beau will know when she finds it."

"So you don't even know what it is you are looking for?" Jordan asked. "Obviously it's a jewel of some sort."

"We presume so." Beau replied.

"I'm not too sure about this whole Beau will know thing though." Avery laughed. "I'm sure she doesn't even know what day of the week it is half the time, her heads so far up in the clouds."

"So where is it you came from?" Beau said, for once ignoring her brother's teasing.

"Well, we live in a small village called Hadleigh with our mum."

Chloe replied. "But we were at Holmes estate with Lord Holmes when we ended up here."

"Lord Holmes?" Avery asked.

"Nee has told us loads of stories about him," Beau replied "But I always thought that they were only stories, in fact I always thought you humans were mythical creatures that didn't exist."''

"Lord Holmes is great!" Bertie the little tapir said with such admiration. "Well put it this way he certainly got Jordan believing in magic."

"I'd say!" Jordan added. "I always thought that you fairies were mythical creatures."

"It looks like we've all been shown a little bit of magic today, we never knew existed." Avery chuckled.

"Yeah and you could do with some of that." Beau laughed at her brother.

"Don't start you sissy!" Avery scowled at Beau, elbowing her hard in the side to shut her up.

Beau bowed her head and did not dare say anything else.

"Who's Nee?" Chloe asked.

"She was my chaperon, the unicorn you saw back at the palace." Beau replied.

"Yes we saw her." Chloe said. "She's beautiful."

"Yes she is." Beau said. "She's looked after me since the day I was born, she's chaperoned so many generations of our family, so she's extra special. Today was the last day she had to look after me."

Beau looked sadly down at the floor and wiped a tear away that was forming in her eye.

Chloe put an arm around Beau and gave her a little squeeze sensing how upset the little fairy must be.

"Look! What's that in the distance?" Bertie said, interrupting their conversation and pointing towards the entrance of a forest.

As they got closer, they saw two funny looking creatures standing next to what looked like an old battered market stall. One was large and quite tubby, with green bobbly looking skin, his hair was grey and balding and he wore an oversized long brown coat. The other one was slightly thinner and younger looking. It also had green bobbly skin and had a funny little tuft of black hair on its head.

"Ah finally we have some customers." The older looking of the two creatures said as he started organising a pile of junk on the market stall.

"Can I interest you in a thing-a-me bob?" He said, thrusting a strange looking object into Avery's face.

"What is it?" Avery asked, curling up his nose at the strange object.

"I told you, it's a thing-a-me bob." The older creature replied, looking as though he didn't even know himself what the object was.

"Maybe not then." He continued, throwing the object away over his shoulder then picking up another. "What about this?"

Avery turned up his nose even more at the dirty, smelly and torn bit of rag the older creature had now shoved under his nose.

"No thanks, I'll pass." He said heaving.

"No, ok let me think then." The older creature said, throwing the bit of rag over his shoulder and picking up yet another even stranger looking object. "Now this is a right bargain."

Beau had meanwhile walked over to look at the objects laid out on the market stall. There were old twisted bits of metal, broken bits of pots, bits of wood and a whole heap of other stuff Beau didn't even recognise.

"It's all junk!" She said, picking up a twisted bit of metal then dropping it again.

"It is not I'll have you know!" The older creature said in a huff. He protectively put his arms over the stuff on the stall as if it were some kind of precious treasure.

"Don't mind him." Said the younger of the creatures. "He gets a bit touchy about his precious items."

"I'd say." Bertie said, looking impatiently at the older creature.

"I'm Veli and that there is Geb." The younger creature said holding out his hand. "It's nice to meet you all."

"Hi! I'm Prince Avery." Replied Avery, stepping forward and shaking Veli's hand. "And this is my sister Princess Beau and our friends Jordan, Chloe and Bertie."

"Nice to meet you." They all said in turn, as they were introduced.

"A prince and princess ay, well I say." Veli said, bowing down. "Did you here that Geb? We're in the company of royalty."

"Yeah! Yeah!" Geb said not paying attention. He was searching through the junk on the stall as if something good would turn up in there somewhere. He picked up one object, studied it and then threw it over his shoulder before picking up another.

"I don't mean to be rude." Beau said. "But what are you?"

"We're Trolls." Veli replied.

"You don't look much like trolls to me." Avery said.

"And you'd know would you?" Geb spat, being quite touchy again.

"No he wouldn't actually." Beau laughed. "He's had his wings for nearly three years and he's never left the palace, he's so lazy."

"No I'm not, I just haven't got round to it yet." Avery stammered.

"More like, it's you that's the sissy!" Beau teased.

"And you're a buffoon!" Geb Grumbled.

"Geb please be nice." Veli said

"But she said my stuff was junk!" Geb grumbled, pointing at Beau.

"Ok, I'm sorry, your stuff is lovely. Honestly!" Beau lied.

"Well that's ok then." Geb said, forcing a smile. "In that case can I interest you in any of these?"

Geb flung open one side of his coat. Hanging inside were twisted forks and spoons and other old battered bits of metal.

"No!" Everyone, including Veli shouted in unison.

"Ok, Ok I get the message." Geb said closing his coat.

"Maybe, if you tried to get some more things." Jordan said, trying to cheer up Geb. "That way you're sure to have something that someone would want."

"I think you might be onto something there." Geb said enthusiastically, now pacing backwards and forwards, scratching his head as though he was thinking of a plan. "I could get bigger and better things, something every creature would want, we could branch out and have stalls in every corner of Dahleigh. We're going to be rich Veli, rich I tell you!"

"Let's not get carried away." Veli laughed.

"But where to get more stuff?" Geb said ignoring Veli, still pacing and scratching his head.

"So what brings you to this neck of the woods?" Veli asked.

"Beau has been sent on a quest." Chloe replied. "She has to find The Jewel of Dahleigh."

"Yes have you heard of it?" Bertie asked.

"Geb! Have you heard of The Jewel of Dahleigh?" Veli shouted at Geb who was still pacing backwards and forwards scratching his head.

Geb stopped shook his head and then continued pacing.

"No sorry we haven't" Veli replied. "What does it look like?"

"We don't know." Avery replied. "We just know that we have to find it for Beau."

Veli looked as confused as everyone else did.

"I know it all sounds odd but that's what we have to do." Beau said seeing the confused look on Veli's face. "Apparently it's my destiny."

Geb sat down on a nearby rock to think for a moment, he was still muttering on about the big plans he had to make them rich. Veli stood behind him and started playfully smoothing down what little hair Geb had.

"I do wish you'd stop doing that!" Geb said impatiently as he flicked Veli's hand away. "Can't you see I'm trying to think?"

"We could be here some time then." Veli joked.

"Why don't you walk with us for a while, we could help you both find some more junk... I mean treasures for your stall." Beau said, obviously still trying to get on the right side of Geb.

"Yes we could all look and that way you could find lots of things." Chloe added.

"Maybe we could help you find out more about this jewel." Veli said.

"Come on then Geb. Let's go with them?" Veli said, starting to smooth down Gebs hair again. "Please!"

Geb flicked Veli's hand away and sighed before looking up at Veli who was batting his eyelids; he then turned to look at the others who were also batting their eyelids all mouthing the words "Please! Please! Please!"

"You never know we might find some other jewels that you could keep for your business." Avery said trying to tempt Geb some more.

"Jewels you say? Now that really could help us with our business. Oh go on then we'll join you." Geb finally agreed as he jumped up and started stuffing as much junk from the stall into his coat. "See I told you we'd be rich one day Veli, didn't I tell you that?"

"Yes Geb you have been saying that my whole life." Veli said rolling his eyes and sighing.

"For now we'll have to try and sell some more of this stuff along the way." Geb said as he continued stuffing artefacts from the stall into his coat.

"As if anyone would buy it." Veli joked under his breath.

Everyone else chuckled.

"What was that?" Geb snapped.

"Oh nothing my dear Geb." Veli laughed. "Nobody said a thing. So come on guys what way are we heading?"

"Through there." Beau replied pointing into the forest.

"We've got to go through that forest?" Chloe said nervously.

"Don't be scared Chloe." Beau said wrapping one arm around Chloe. "Dahleigh is a beautiful and safe place, nothing bad ever happens here."

"How would you know?" Avery snapped. "This is the first time you've ever been out of the palace."

"Look who's talking!" Beau snapped back. "Look mum and dad have always said what a safe beautiful place the rest of Dahleigh is and you know they would never put us in danger."

"I suppose..." Avery replied nervously

"Come on you lot!" Bertie shouted, as he had now started walking into the forest. "I haven't got all day!"

"Bit touchy isn't he." Geb said before following Bertie into the forest. His coat dragging along the floor with the weight of all the things he had stuffed into it and making a clanging sound as he walked.

"He's a fine one to talk." Veli laughed as he followed Geb.

"They make me laugh." Beau said, grabbing hold of Chloe's hand and skipping after the trolls. "Come on lets go."

Avery and Jordan just stood still for a moment and watched the others walking into the forest.

"Well I suppose it's down to us two to baby sit this lot." Avery said to Jordan, crossing his arms and laughing.

"Tell me about it." Jordan laughed, before they both followed everyone else into the forest.

The Wailing Tree

"Wow! It's breathtaking." Chloe said as they walked deeper into the forest. "And I thought the forest back at The Estate was enchanting."

Chloe stopped for a moment to take in the scenery. All around her was the most enchanting forest you could ever imagine. The trees were all different colours and all baring different exotic flowers and fruits, some of which Chloe had never seen before. The shrubs and bushes were covered with berries of all shapes and colours. On the forest bed lay a blanket of soft purple grass with toadstools that popped up in various places. Birds of every shade of the rainbow sang from the trees and the forest was alive with insects and other wildlife. It was the most stunningly vibrant place Chloe had ever seen.

Even Beau and Avery looked in complete awe at the forest that they had only ever looked at out of the palace windows every day.

"I always knew it would be beautiful in here." Beau said. "But I never imagined it would be quite so beautiful."

"Me either." Avery added.

"We've lived in this forest my whole life." Veli said also admiring his surroundings. "And it just gets more and more breathtaking every day."

"I always imagined trolls to be big nasty creatures." Jordan said looking from Veli to Geb.

"No not us." Veli replied.

"Are other trolls nasty then?" Chloe asked.

"To be honest I couldn't tell you." Veli replied "We're the only two trolls around here. "But, D... Geb says that trolls are brave and courageous, he says there are more out there but they live far away in another part of Dahleigh. Isn't that right Geb?"

Geb didn't reply. He was busy scouring the forest floor for treasures, every now and then he picked something up and studied it very closely before shoving it into his coat and picking up another object.

"Haven't you ever wanted to go and find them?" Avery asked.

"Well I have but Geb has never been so keen on the idea." Veli replied. "He says we do just fine on our own."

"I wouldn't want to leave the forest if I lived here." Jordan said still looking totally in awe by his surroundings. "I wish mum were here to see this and not back at The Estate."

"Where is The Estate?" Geb asked, still picking up objects from the floor, studying them with interest and then shoving them in his coat.

"That's where we were before we got sucked into the painting." Jordan replied.

"What do you mean? Sucked into a painting?" Avery asked looking totally bemused.

"Exactly what I said; we got sucked into a painting." Jordan replied.

"Maybe you should start from the beginning." Bertie suggested.

"Good idea." Beau said, also looking completely confused. "Let's sit down and rest for a while so Jordan and Chloe can tell us all about it."

"Good idea." Veli said walking over to a patch of purple grass and sitting down. "My feet hurt."

Everyone followed Veli and sat down to listen to the children explain how they ended up in Dahleigh.

"Well what happened." Chloe began.

"I'll tell the story!" Jordan butted in. "Well what happened is... We won a competition for a day out at Holmes Estate..."

"That's a big house in the country that has a safari park and everything on its grounds." Chloe interrupted rather enthusiastically.

"As I was saying..." Jordan continued, as he gave Chloe a disapproving look. "We won this competition and the next day we were being picked up and taken to Devon with our mum, where Lord Holmes..."

"He's this great old man that lives there." Chloe interrupted again.

Jordan gave Chloe another disapproving look.

"Lord Holmes..." He continued once more. "As she said lives at Holmes Estate, well he showed us around his whole estate. That is after Albert took us exploring in The Forest."

"Albert was our chauffer, I really liked him." Chloe interrupted yet again. Bertie grinned to himself.

"What's a chauffer?" Geb asked.

"It's a person that drives people around in a big fancy car." Bertie replied.

"What's a car?" Geb asked.

"It's a big metal thing with wheels." Bertie replied impatiently, he was trying to make his answer as simple as possible so Jordan could continue with his story.

"As I was saying..." Jordan said. "Lord Holmes also showed us his lovely big manor house. Inside were loads of paintings. One minute we were in his nursery studying one of his paintings, the next we were being sucked into it. Everything went blank for a while and then there we were, stood in front of loads of fairies. It was mad."

"How exciting!" Veli said in amazement.

"So you come from a world called Holmes Estate?" Geb asked.

"No!" Jordan said trying not to laugh. "Holmes Estate is just the name of the place; it's in Great Britain, which is a little island on earth. So I suppose you'd call our world The Earth."

"Wow! The Earth." Veli cooed, looking as though he were trying to imagine what it would be like. "I should like to visit there one day."

"You said your mum was with you." Beau said. "What's she like and why didn't she get sucked into the painting?"

"Our mum's great!" Jordan replied. "She does everything for us and she is so much fun."

"I miss her." Chloe began to sob. "We've never been anywhere without her before."

"Chloe please don't cry." Bertie said. "I promise you Lord Holmes will look after her."

"But she must be so worried about us!" Chloe said now wailing.

"Look she knows that your safe and where you are." Bertie continued, as he patted Chloe's hand with his paw to try to calm her down. "Lord Holmes had a talk with her when you were off exploring the forest without her."

"How do you know we went for a walk without them?" Jordan asked a puzzled look on his face.

Bertie froze for a second.

"I didn't. I um….." He stammered, before another wailing sound interrupted him.

"Chloe stop crying now!" Jordan said impatiently. "Bertie told you mum was ok."

"It's not me." Chloe said.

They all sat up and looked around the forest to see where the noise was coming from.

"It sounds like its coming from over there." Geb said pointing towards some trees.

They all stood up and nervously crept towards the sound that was getting louder and louder. When they got to a huge tree, they stopped.

"It's coming from in there." Veli said pointing at the tree.

"Hello in there!" Geb shouted at the tree, before placing his ear against the trunk. "Are you ok?"

The wailing got even louder.

"I can't believe that tree's making all that noise." Geb continued now knocking at the tree with his knuckles.

"It's not coming from the tree you imbecile!" Bertie said. "It's coming from behind the tree."

They all huddled together and slowly peered around the tree. Sitting at the base of it was a tiny, tiny pixie. Her head buried into her hands and she was crying uncontrollably.

"Aw the poor little thing, it's only a baby it must be lost." Geb said finally showing his softer side. He walked over to the pixie, that wasn't even the size of his foot, and knelt down.

"Come here little pixie, stop crying." He said as he put his hand out to try to comfort it. The little pixie stopped crying instantly and opened its mouth wide and without warning, it clamped its teeth down hard on Geb's finger.

"Get it off! Get it off!" Geb wailed, his eyes watering with the pain.

The pixie kept its teeth tightly clamped together.

"What a naughty little pixie you are!" Chloe said in a stern voice. "Now let go!"

The pixie let go of Geb's finger and started wailing again.

"Oh sorry, I didn't mean to make you cry." Chloe said guiltily. "But you were hurting my friend."

Geb was now holding up his throbbing finger, his eyes still watering with the pain. "That hurt!" He grumbled.

"Well what do you expect, with those big clod hoppers coming towards her, you probably frightened the poor little thing?" Veli said walking over to Geb and standing behind him. He started playfully smoothing down Gebs' little bit of hair again.

"Would you get off!" Geb shouted, swatting Veli's hand away. He then walked off and sat down in a sulk with his back turned on a nearby rock, still holding onto his throbbing finger.

"Come here little pixie we won't hurt you." Beau said in a gentle voice and holding out her hands to the pixie, that was small enough to fit into the palm of them.

The pixie jumped onto Beau's hands and looked up at her with big, sad, puppy dog eyes.

"Don't be scared little one!" Beau said

"Pretty Fairy." The pixie said in a babyish voice, pointing at Beau.

"Aw thank you." Beau replied. "My name is Beau."

"She's so sweet!" Chloe cooed, peering at the little pixie. "Hi, I'm Chloe."

"Me KC." The little pixie said prodding herself in the chest.

"It's nice to meet you KC." Beau said. "That other fairy over there is my brother Avery, and that's Jordan." Beau pointed in their direction.

Avery and Jordan both stepped forward and said hello.

"And that there is Bertie." Beau continued as she pointed at the little tapir. Bertie stepped forward.

"It's nice to meet you." He said.

KC jumped up and down with excitement when she saw the little tapir step forward.

"She likes you." Chloe laughed, looking down at Bertie.

"Hello, little one." Veli said stepping forward. "My name is Veli and that grumpy oaf over there is Geb, We're trolls."

Geb who was still sitting on the rock with his back turned, nursing his finger, turned around and grunted at the little pixie.

KC huffed and blew a raspberry at him. Geb grumbled and turned away again.

"Don't mind him." Veli laughed. "He's always grumpy."

KC chuckled and did a grumpy impression of Geb.

Everyone except Geb laughed.

"Are you lost little one?" Beau asked looking down at the little pixie stood in the palm of her hands.

KC nodded

"Lost Kipsie." She said

"Poor little thing." Beau said. "Is Kipsie your friend?"

KC Shook her head.

"Is Kipsie your pet then?" Asked Veli.

KC shook her head again.

"No! Ok is she your sister?" Chloe asked.

KC nodded her head, her bottom lip started to tremble as if she were about to cry again.

"Please don't cry." Beau said gently. "You can come with us and we can help you find her."

KC smiled sweetly at Beau and hugged her thumb.

"You can ride on Bertie's' back." Chloe said, gently taking KC from Beau's hands and placing her on Bertie's' back.

"That's ok I'm used to chauffeuring people around." Bertie grumbled under his breath.

"What was that Bertie?" Chloe asked not hearing what he had said.

"Nothing!" Bertie lied. "I didn't say a word."

"Come on you lot!" Both Avery and Jordan shouted together. They had already started to walk further into the forest.

"Ok we're coming!" Shouted Beau as they all started to follow Avery and Jordan.

"Are you coming Geb?" Veli called back to Geb who was still sitting on the rock.

Geb grumbled something under his breath and remained seated on the rock.

"Come on Geb. Please." Chloe called back.

"No!" Geb said stubbornly as he still nursed his throbbing finger.

Jordan stopped and looked back at Geb and rolled his eyes. He then picked up an object from the floor and walked back to where Geb was seated.

"Look at this." Jordan said showing Geb the useless object he had just picked up. "This would be great for your business.

Geb snatched the object and studied it.

"If you come with us you can find more stuff like that." Jordan said trying to tempt Geb to change his mind.

"He's right you know Geb." Veli said walking over to them both. "After all, that was the whole point of us being here."

"I suppose." Geb sighed.

"And I like being here with our new friends," Veli said looking at all the new friends they had made. "Come on its been so long since we've seen anyone else, I'm not saying I'm bored with your company or anything, it's just nice to talk to someone else, plus I want to hear more about earth and Lord Holmes and beau's quest."

"Ok! Ok I'll come then. Only if you keep that little THING! Away from me." Geb replied pointing at KC.

KC turned and blew a raspberry at Geb, who growled back at KC before standing up and following everyone. As he walked, his coat that was now even more weighed down with the junk he had collected made a loud clanging noise.

"I'm surprised he can still move with all that junk in there." Bertie laughed.

"Tell me about it." Veli chuckled as he rolled his eyes at Geb.

The Naughty Nymph

As they walked further into the forest Veli, Avery and Jordan talked amongst themselves while Geb walked beside them searching the floor for yet more junk to stuff into his oversized coat. Chloe and Beau walked either side of Bertie singing silly songs to KC who was still riding upon Bertie's back.

"Look at this Veli." Geb said, picking up a long twisted bit of metal and showing it to Veli.

"Yes Geb it's lovely." Veli replied, not even looking at the object that Geb was now stuffing into his coat.

Geb Nervously approached KC, who was still sat upon Bertie's back.

"Can I interest you in a wazzit?" He said opening his coat and smiling to try to make amends with the little pixie.

KC blew him a raspberry and then gnashed her teeth at him.

"Why you horrid little..." Geb said jumping backwards. "I was only trying to be nice."

"I don't think she likes you very much." Bertie laughed.

"Well I don't like her much either." Geb grumbled, holding up his very sore looking finger again.

They all walked on in silence for a while, looking around the enchanted forest.

"Ah young man." Geb said casually strolling over to Jordan and flinging open his coat. "I'm sure there's something you'd be interested in now."

"No thanks!" Jordan said curling up his nose at the objects hanging from Geb's coat.

"Don't you get tired lugging all that stuff around?" Avery laughed at all the things hanging from the Trolls coat.

"Oh no! Not a big strong Troll like me" Geb said puffing out his chest. "I'm..."

Geb was interrupted by a high-pitched giggling sound coming from a nearby bush.

"What was that?" Chloe asked, nervously grabbing hold of Beau's hand.

"It's probably just a bird you Sissy!" Jordan teased.

Chloe and Beau both looked disapprovingly at Jordan.

"Boys!" They both said together.

Once again, there was a giggling sound coming from the bush.

"I'm scared." Both Chloe and Beau said at the same time as they grabbed each other tighter.

Both Jordan and Avery grinned and looked at each other, they both mimed the same word. "Sissy's!"

"I'll go and see what it is." Geb said puffing out his chest. "I'm a Troll, I'm not scared."

Geb marched towards the bush, hesitated then all of a sudden looked very nervous.

"Jeese, I'll go." Veli said pushing Geb aside. "I am a big brave troll too you know."

Veli walked over to the bush and jumped out of his skin when a funny little creature that looked rather like a pixie only bigger, leapt out from behind the bush. Veli stumbled backwards and fell to the floor.

"Big brave Troll is you?" The creature said chuckling. "More like a green-bellied goblin."

"I most certainly am not!" Veli huffed, trying to get up off the floor.

The creature jumped on top of Veli preventing him from getting up.

"My you are a handsome goblin." She said fluttering her eyelids at Veli and stroking his hair with one hand.

"Get off me you horrible Nymph!" Veli shouted, pushing the creature away.

"I'm an Oceanid actually." The Nymph replied as she pinned Veli to floor again. "Look I have scales."

The nymph thrust her arm into Veli's face before stroking his hair again.

Indeed, she did have greenish coloured scales all over her body.

"An Oceanid is a water nymph." Veli replied, in a very matter of fact way. He pushed the nymphs hand away. "Now would you get off me woman!"

Veli was trying relentlessly to push the Nymph off and clamber to his feet. But the nymph continued to pin him down.

Everyone else just stood smiling at the entertaining scene going on in front of them.

"He likes me." The nymph said hugging Veli, who was now getting very impatient.

"No I do not. You're an annoying, horrible, ugly little nymph." Veli shouted again pushing the nymph away.

"Oceanid." The nymph reminded Veli. "I can tell that you're impressed."

"Ah! You are really bugging me." Veli yelled putting his hands over his ears.

"Aw, he loves me." The nymph said dreamily. "The goblin loves me."

"I do not! And I'm not a goblin I'm a troll." Veli shouted right into the nymphs face. "And my name's Veli."

Everyone else was by now in fits of laughter. The Nymph had once again snuggled up close to Veli and was stroking his hair again looking up at him with her huge green eyes fluttering her long eyelashes at him.

"Geb sort her out. Please!" Veli pleaded, looking helplessly at Geb.

Geb was now rolling around on the floor he was laughing so much. All the junk in his coat was crashing together and falling out all over the floor.

"Hello." Prince Avery said trying not to laugh anymore and stepping forward to try to help save Veli. "I'm Prince Avery."

"Hello Prince Avery. I'm Doris." The nymph replied as she jumped off of Veli and curtsied gracefully at the prince.

"Can I interest you in any of today's bargains?" Geb said shoving Avery aside and flinging open his coat. "I'm Geb by the way."

"Is he for sale?" Doris asked pointing at Veli and fluttering her eyelids again.

"No I am not!" Veli snapped as he finally got to his feet and brushed himself off.

"Hello my dear." Bertie said trying to change the subject for Veli's sake. "My name is Bertie and these are our other friends Jordan, Princess Beau, Chloe and my little friend back there is KC."

Everyone said hello to Doris.

"Oh and you've already met Veli there." Bertie added laughing and nodding his head towards Veli.

"Oh yes the handsome one." Doris replied. She darted over to Veli and started to stroke his hair again.

"Right that's it. I've had enough of this!" Veli shouted, slapping Doris's hand away. "I'm off!"

Veli started to stomp off into the forest. Doris ran after him and snatched the battered old guitar out of his hand.

"Give that back right now! You… You… Squid lips!" He shouted.

Doris poked out her tongue and ran away from Veli.

"Why you little…" Veli began as he stormed after Doris. "I'm going to get you."

"Ooh! Come and get me then, you handsome beast." Doris said turning and flirtatiously wiggling her hips as she waved Veli's guitar in front of her.

Veli leapt forward to try to snatch the guitar but Doris darted behind a tree before he had a chance to reach it. Veli fell flat on his face and everyone burst into fits of laughter again.

Veli stood up, his face now brilliant red with anger.

"Aw! Did that hurt?" Doris mocked. "Can I kiss it better?"

"Don't you come near me you squid lips!" Veli said screwing up his face in disgust.

"Don't you want this back then, you green-bellied goblin?" Doris asked waving the guitar out in front of her again. Veli thrust out his hand to try to grab the guitar yet again.

"Ah! Ah! Ah!" Doris said snatching the guitar back and hiding it behind her back. "You've got to give me a kiss first."

Doris puckered up her lips, closed her eyes and waited for Veli to give her a kiss.

"Forget it!" Veli said screwing his face up again. "I'm not kissing THAT!"

"Oh go on, give her a kiss." Geb teased, rolling around on the floor again laughing.

"Yeah go on." Doris said puckering up her lips again. "You know you want to."

"No I do not!" Veli said now getting very impatient. "Oh forget the guitar!"

Veli turned and walked away.

"Oh here you go then." Doris huffed as she handed him the guitar. "But I know you wanted to kiss me really."

Veli snatched his guitar back and cradled it like a baby.

Everyone had now stopped laughing and was picking themselves up off the floor for the second time.

"Come on you lot, can we get going again now!" Veli said, obviously trying to get away from Doris.

"I'm so tired." Chloe yawned as she got up.

"Me too." Beau added.

"It is getting late." Bertie said looking up at the sky that now had thousands of stars twinkling like diamonds and three pink moons that set the whole forest aglow.

"Maybe we should settle down here for the night." Avery said.

"We can set off again at daybreak."

"Good idea!" Geb said. "Maybe we should find a tree to shelter under."

"I know a good place." Doris said enthusiastically. "That is... if you don't mind me tagging along?"

"Of course we don't mind." Beau said. "The more the merrier."

"Well I mind!" Veli huffed. "I don't want to put up with that... that... squid lips!"

"Oh be quiet." Doris said striking her cheek against Veli's cheek. "You love me really."

"Yuk! Get off." Veli said pushing her off and wiping his cheek. "If you insist on tagging along with us then I suggest you stay away from me."

"I know you don't really mean that." Doris said blowing Veli a kiss. "Come on everyone this way!"

Doris darted off between two trees.

Everyone followed Doris to a magnificent blue weeping willow that stood in the centre of a clearing in the forest.

"Wow!" Jordan cooed looking up at the huge tree. "Good job Doris."

"I know, isn't it beautiful?" Doris said looking rather pleased with herself. "Not as beautiful as me though, isn't that right Veli?"

Doris looked up at Veli and batted her eyelids.

"In your dreams, squid lips!" Veli grumbled as he gave Doris a disapproving look.

"I often stay here in this tree." Doris said, ignoring Veli's comment. "It's one of my favourite places to sit."

Veli set about making a fire in a bid to keep as far away from Doris as he could while the others made themselves comfortable and started telling Doris about Beau's quest and how the children had ended up in Dahleigh and also how they had come to meet Geb, Veli and KC.

"Wow! What an exciting day you've had." Doris said once they had finished telling the story. "And what an adventure it's going to be. I can't wait!"

"Oh brother!" Veli sighed as he rolled his eyes at Doris. He had now joined the others sat around the fire he had just made.

"And not only have I met some great new friends, I have found the love of my life." Doris continued as she jumped up and threw herself down on Veli's lap, one hand stroking his hair again and the other plucking at the guitar strings.

"So do you play?" She added in a husky tone.

Veli pushed her off his lap and cradled his guitar again.

"Of course I do." He replied grumpily.

"Oh play us a song Veli." Chloe requested. "Please!"

"Oh yes please do!" Avery said.

"Play song!" KC added in her babyish little voice. She was no longer sat upon Bertie's back, and was now curled up on Beau's lap.

Doris had now settled herself down next to Chloe. She rested her chin on her hands and looked dreamily at Veli waiting for him to play them a song on his guitar.

Veli tucked the guitar under his arm and started playing a soothing lullaby. Gradually one by one, the fairies, the children, the pixie, one troll and the nymph fell fast asleep. When it was only himself and Bertie still awake, he stopped playing.

"Aw look at the little darlings." Veli said looking down at them all. "I'm so pleased we bumped into you all today."

"Yes, there not a bad lot really." Bertie replied also looking at all the others sleeping.

"Yeah, well, most of them are ok." Veli said as he looked grumpily at Doris. "Others are a little harder to cope with."

"Oh she's only teasing!" Bertie said chuckling at Veli. "She does really like you though."

"Tell me about it." Veli huffed. "She's really annoying; I can't believe she's going to be tagging along with us"

"Oh you've just got to learn how to handle her." Bertie laughed. "She seems harmless."

"Well the only thing I'll be handling on her is her neck when I wring it!" Veli joked.

"That's more like it!" Bertie giggled. "Although I doubt you need to go quite that far,"

"Well as long as she stays away from me, she'll do fine." Veli sighed.

"I'm sure you can handle her." Bertie said as he smiled down at Doris who was now talking in her sleep saying Veli's name over and over again.

"Well we better get some sleep too." Veli said yawning and stretching out his arms. "We have a long day ahead of us tomorrow."

"Yes we should." Bertie replied. "I wonder what surprises tomorrow will have in store?"

"Who knows?" Veli replied. "No more horrid little nymphs I hope!"

"Well I'm going to go and sleep over there." Bertie said pointing at some thick bushes nearby. "Nice and secluded."

Veli looked at Bertie slightly puzzled.

"Um...Well, us Tapirs are a bit fussy about sleeping in big groups you see." Bertie quickly added before he stood up and disappeared into the bushes.

"Strange little thing" Veli said to himself before lying down on a soft bit of grass and falling asleep.

The Nutty Tree

At daybreak the next morning, under the magnificent blue weeping willow, nine friends stirred to the sound of birds singing to the morning sunrise. An early morning mist hovered mystically over the forest bed and the early morning breeze danced gracefully around the trees making them rustle and sway slightly. Bertie had now re-emerged from his secluded spot in the bushes and had rejoined the group.

"Wow it looks even more enchanting now!" Chloe said sleepily, as she sat up and looked around rubbing her eyes.

Everyone else sat up and looked around at the eerie yet breathtaking views around them.

"Hold on a minute, Where's Geb?" Veli said now looking in the direction where Geb had fallen asleep the night before. "And what is that!?"

Everyone turned to look at a huge rock that was covered with blue glitter, where Geb should have been.

"Pretty impressive huh!" A voice came from up in the weeping willow.

Everybody jumped and looked up.

"Chi!" Beau squealed, jumping to her feet and grinning from ear to ear. "What are you doing here?"

"You do realise you're not meant to leave our kingdom for at least a month after you get your colour." Avery said, looking rather annoyed to see Chi. "You're going to get into so much trouble."

"He does have a point you know Chi." Beau said. "So what are you doing here?"

"Well it's like this..." Chi started as he flew down from the tree and sat down with everyone. "I don't know whether you noticed but my father wasn't at the ceremony."

"No I didn't notice." Beau replied. "But with everything that happened at the Ceremony I didn't think, sorry."

"Was he meant to be there then?" Avery asked grumpily.

"Yes he was and I know he wouldn't have missed it for the world." Chi continued. "When he still hadn't arrived back by late last night I started to get really worried so I snuck out to look for him."

"That still doesn't explain how you ended up here!" Avery asked still sounding fed up that Chi was there.

"Well... um... the bottom line is... I got lost." Chi replied. "I got a bit carried away scattering my fairy dust you see. I lost the path I was on. It was only by chance that I stumbled across you lot."

"Lucky more like it." Beau said frowning. "Chi you could have been hurt."

"I know but I'm so worried about my dad." Chi said, now looking quite scared. "I just have a bad feeling, I know he goes away a lot but he would never have missed the colouring ceremony, I know it."

Beau put her arm around Chi's shoulders to comfort him.

"He'll be ok!" She said to try to reassure her friend. "I'm sure he will."

"Anyway as I was saying." Chi said as he tried to force a smile. "When I stumbled across you lot I thought I'd hang about and surprise you. So... SURPRISE!"

"Well you certainly did that." Beau said jumping up and down with excitement and hugging her friend. "I'm so pleased to see you."

"I see you've picked up a few strays." Chi said looking at everyone that Beau and Avery had met along the way.

Beau laughed and one by one introduced each of them.

"There is meant to be one more, Geb." Avery added after Beau had finished introducing the rest. "But he seems to have disappeared."

"Yes I wonder where he's got to." Veli said scratching his head and looking around.

The glitter-covered rock began to move and startled everyone.

"That's not a rock!" Chloe gasped. "It's Geb."

"Have I missed anything?" Geb said sleepily as he sat up and rubbed his eyes.

Everyone burst into fits of laughter at the sight of Geb sitting there covered in blue glitter.

"Oops! I thought it was an ugly old rock." Chi laughed. "So I tried brightening it up a bit."

"Do I look like a rock?" Geb grumbled looking down at his glitter-covered body. "And who are you?"

Geb rubbed his eyes and took a second look at Chi to check he wasn't seeing things.

"This is my best friend Chi." Beau said.

"And you must be Geb? It's nice to meet you." Chi said holding out his hand.

Geb rubbed his eyes once more and then shook Chi's' little hand.

"Hold on a minute, how'd you know my name?" He said.

"Oh go back to sleep Geb." Veli laughed, stepping up behind Geb and playfully stroking his hair again.

"Uh, what?" Geb said swatting Veli's hand away.

He obviously hadn't realised that Chi had been there a while.

"Please do wake up a bit Geb." Bertie sighed.

Geb didn't reply and sat sleepily brushing the fairy dust from his body.

"So are you going to go home now?" Avery asked Chi trying to get rid of him.

"No he is not!" Beau scowled at her brother.

"But he's got to go home!" He shouted back. "He shouldn't be here!"

"But he might get lost again!" Beau shouted even louder.

"Please! Calm down you two!" Bertie shouted. "You're frightening poor little KC."

KC had now jumped onto Bertie's back and was hiding behind his ear trembling.

"Please Avery, can't I stay with you?" Chi asked looking pleadingly into Avery's eyes. "I'm too scared to go back on my own."

Avery didn't say anything for a second but he knew he couldn't really send him back alone.

"Oh go on then." He finally said. "But you've got to do as I! Say."

"Yippee! I promise you won't regret this." Chi squealed.."

"Woo hoo." Doris yelled with excitement, despite, not really knowing Chi that well.

"Oh be quite you." Veli sighed.

"Give me a kiss then handsome and I might." Doris replied as she slid over to Veli and started stroking his hair.

"I told you I'm not kissing those squid lips!" Veli said pushing her away.

"And I told you that deep down there somewhere, you do really want to give us a kiss." Doris replied.

All of a sudden, Veli's tummy made a huge rumbling sound.

"See I told you." Doris said jumping back over to Veli and now stroking his stomach.

"I'm hungry! You brainless, annoying, smelly little nymph." Veli shouted as he gave Doris one last hard shove away from him.

"Yes we should all eat really." Bertie said. "Before we carry on with the quest."

"But we don't have anything to eat." Avery said.

"Duh! Look around you." Chi said playfully knocking Avery on the head. "The forest is full of food."

"You wait there you lot!" He said as he flapped his wings and flew up into the trees. "Leave it to me. I'll get our breakfast."

"I can't believe we've been landed with another annoying little brat." Avery grumbled quietly to Jordan. "We've had it now he's here; they are both nightmares when they're together."

"And with Chloe that makes three nightmares." Jordan laughed.

"Right here we go." Chi called minutes later as he reappeared from the trees with his arms full of all kinds of exotic fruits and berries. "Tuck in everyone!"

Everyone sat down and grabbed some fruit to eat. While they sat there, Beau told Chi everything that had happened so far.

Once they had all finished eating they set off on their way again.

They all walked further into the forest chatting amongst themselves. Beau and Chi were telling Chloe and Doris about the Palace and all the adventures they had planned together. Jordan and Avery were complaining about the girls and Chi. Bertie, who had KC on his back was talking to Veli about Lord Holmes and The Estate and Geb was walking on ahead scouring the forest for objects he could stuff into his coat and try and sell later on. He did turn once to open his coat for Chi to buy something but Beau stopped him before he had a chance to.

"No Geb he isn't interested in buying anything." Beau said, interrupting Geb's sales pitch.

"I'll show you lot!" He grumbled. "One day someone will buy something from me, and I'll prove it's not all junk!"

Geb stomped off ahead again and disappeared around a bend. By the time, everyone else had made it around the corner Geb was standing facing a tree looking as though he were talking to it.

"If you buy this ma'am…" Geb said to the tree holding up one of his objects. "I'll let you have another free."

"I'm starting to get worried about him." Veli said under his breath to Bertie. "He's even trying to flog his stuff to the trees now."

They all approached Geb who was now pulling more junk from

his coat and showing it to the tree.

"Geb! What are you doing?" Bertie said with a puzzled look on his face.

"Or maybe I can interest you in this?" Geb said ignoring Bertie and holding up yet another object in front of the tree.

Suddenly the tree moved causing everyone except Geb to jump.

"Ooh! What a bargain." The tree said in a loud, high-pitched eccentric voice. "I'll take it!"

The tree reached out one of its lower braches and took the object from Geb.

"Really! That's great." Geb said not quite believing himself that someone had finally took interest in his stuff.

The tree had green silvery bark, big bright red lips and huge blue eyes. It didn't have any leaves or fruit or flowers just curly branched that had what looked like some kind of weird jewels hanging from them. The tree added the object to its branches.

"What do you think?" The tree said to Geb posing to show off her new accessory. "Does it suit me?"

"It's simply marvellous my dear!" Geb boomed enthusiastically.

"That tree can talk!" Chloe finally said in shock, looking up at the tree with her mouth wide open in amazement.

"Of course I can talk silly." The tree replied loudly. "I'm Penny, the nutty tree."

"See I told you my stuff wasn't junk!" Geb said proudly to himself. "Thank you Penny. My name's Geb."

Geb went on to introduce everyone else, who in turn stepped forward and said hello.

"No Geb Thank you." Penny said shaking her branches so the jewels made a jingling sound. "I do love a bargain."

"And you have an eye for one I see." Geb said admiring Penny's branches more closely.

The jewels that were hanging from her branches were in fact bits of junk and Geb was now looking in total awe at them.

"Why thank you. Do you like it?" Penny said shaking her branches again.

"It's the most amazing thing I have ever seen!" Geb replied in complete awe.

"You're the most amazing thing I've ever seen." Doris interrupted tucking her head under Veli's chin and looking up at him fluttering her eyelids.

"Well you're the ugliest thing I've ever seen!" Veli grumbled pushing Doris away.

Everyone chuckled at Veli who was beginning to look more and more fed up by Doris annoying him.

"I could use someone like you to help me with my new venture." Geb said to penny. "Someone with an eye for a bargain."

"What? You mean help you sell your stuff?" Penny asked

looking quite interested at the prospect.

"Yes and help us find more stock." Geb replied. "As I said you do seem to have an eye for a bargain, and I'm sure this lot won't mind you coming along"

"Of course we don't mind." Beau answered for everyone as she smiled sweetly up at Penny. "It's not as if we haven't already picked up a few extras on the way already."

"But I have an eye for a bargain." Veli interrupted, sounding quite put out by Geb's comment. "Not to say that I mind Penny coming along or anything, it's just…"

"Yes and I'm that bargain he has an eye for." Doris butted in, in a dreamy voice looking up at Veli.

"No offence Veli…" Geb said ignoring Doris's little comment. "I know it's always just been you and me, but Penny could really help us BOTH with this, be honest your hearts never quite been in it has it? All you seem to care about is that guitar."

"And me!" Doris added.

Veli looked down at his guitar and protectively cradled it.

"But you made me this when I was a wee troll." He said also ignoring Doris. "I love my guitar."

"And me." Doris added again prodding herself in the chest.

"I know you do. Love the guitar that is." Geb said throwing Doris a glance. "And there's nothing wrong with that. It's just I have plans, big plans and I think that with Penny's help we could be rich Veli, rich I say."

"See there you go again always getting carried away. It's always been the same my whole life." Veli grumbled. "You and your silly dreams!"

"Look it's ok to have a dream." Chi said as he walked over to Veli and placed his small hand on Veli's arm. "Geb has a dream and really you should be encouraging it. Besides you don't know until you try and who knows one day that dream might just come true and if not at least you can say you tried."

Veli looked down at the floor for a moment and sighed.

"I suppose you're right." He said quietly before looking up at Penny and smiling. "So then Penny, are you in?"

"Help you sniff out a bargain!" Penny squealed with excitement. "Are you kidding, of course I'm in?"

Geb smiled proudly at Veli.

"Well then, what are we waiting for?" Penny said loudly. "Let's go!"

Penny lifted up her giant roots and started to walk further into the forest in the direction everyone had been heading before they had stopped to talk to her. All the friends followed again chatting amongst themselves while Geb went on ahead with Penny so they could both look for bargains together. As they walked, Geb told her about the quest and the adventures they had had so far.

The Silver Lake

"This forest goes on forever." Beau moaned. "We've been walking for hours."

"My feet hurt." Chloe then moaned.

"My feet and my wings ache." Chi added.

"Oh be quiet you lot!" Avery snapped at them.

Everyone was feeling totally exhausted, they had been walking through the forest for hours and still they had not made it through to the silver lake on the other side.

"Penny, do you know if we're nearly there?" Bertie asked. "After all you are a tree."

"Not far now." Penny replied.

"Well then, we'll press on and rest when we get out of here." Bertie said.

Everyone sighed in unison and carried on walking in silence.

"Almost there." Penny said after about another ten minutes.

Just up ahead everyone could see an opening in the trees and could just catch the glow coming from the silver lake. Instantly everyone perked up and started chatting again.

"Ello handsome." Doris said skipping over to Veli. "You ready for that kiss yet?"

"Go away squid lips!" Veli huffed.

"I think she's got a serious crush on you." Penny laughed.

"Leave it out." Veli replied as he strolled on faster ahead of everyone else.

"Penny, look at this?" Geb said as he picked up a large flat golden object from the floor.

"Wow! It's beautiful." Penny cooed as she studied the object in Geb's hand.

"Then you should have it." Geb replied. "Hang it on one of your branches."

"No I couldn't." Penny replied pushing the object away. "We need it for the business."

"I insist. It would look lovely up there." Geb said pointing to a space on Penny's branches.

Penny blushed, took the object and hung it from the branch Geb had just pointed too.

"How does it look?" She asked, shaking her branches so everything jingled together.

"Superb!" Geb replied.

They were suddenly interrupted by a loud shouting, so loud everyone had to put their hands over their ears.

"What on earth was that?" Jordan said frowning, his hands still over his ears

"KC!" Came the very loud shout again.

KC, who had been sleeping on Bertie's back suddenly jumped up with excitement.

"Kipsie!" She squealed

Just up ahead near an opening in the trees they could just make out two tiny creatures wandering around. Every now and then, they were putting their heads into a bush and then reemerging shaking their heads.

"KC!" Came the loud shouting yet again.

Everyone once again had to put their hands back over their ears. KC jumped off Bertie's back and ran towards the two little figures.

"Kipsie! Kipsie!" She shrieked. She shrieked so loud everyone jumped to put their hands back over their ears for the third time.

"How can something so small be so loud?" Geb grumbled.

Everyone walked over to join KC who was now standing with another little pixie that was slightly bigger than her and a little elf that was the same size as the bigger pixie.

"Found Kipsie." KC said pointing at the other pixie.

"Yes I'm Kipsie." The pixie said. "Thank you for finding my little sister and taking care of her."

"That's ok." Beau replied. "It was our pleasure."

"Pretty fairy Beau." KC said now pointing up at Beau.

"Well it wasn't my pleasure." Geb interrupted holding up his sore finger. "You should keep that thing! In a cage."

"Geb nasty fat troll!" KC snapped and then blew a raspberry at Geb.

"KC. be nice!" Kipsie snapped at her little sister. "They have all been nice enough to take care of you."

KC cowered away from Kipsie and looked shamefully down at the floor.

"Sorry Geb." Kipsie continued. "She can be a naughty little thing at times."

"I'd say!" Geb replied. Holding up his sore finger again.

"Well you were waving those clod-hoppers in her face." Veli laughed. "Hi! I'm Veli; it's nice to meet you."

"And I'm Doris!" Doris said barging between Kipsie and Veli. "I'm his girlfriend."

"No she is not!" Veli snapped. "She's an ugly little nymph!"

"He is really." Doris whispered to Kipsie. "He just doesn't realise it yet."

"It's nice to meet you Doris." Kipsie laughed.

"Bertie my friend." KC said jumping onto Bertie's back and giving him a huge hug.

"It's nice to meet you Bertie." Kipsie said. "I do hope she hasn't been any trouble."

"Not at all." Bertie replied. "She's a cute little thing really."

"Very cute." Chloe added. "Hi I'm Chloe and this is my brother Jordan."

Jordan knelt down to say hello to the little pixie.

"Pretty tree." KC said pointing up at Penny.

"Hello." Kipsie said nervously looking up at the huge tree towering above her.

"Please don't be scared, I won't hurt you." Penny said smiling sweetly down at kipsie. "I'm Penny."

"Lastly this is my brother Prince Avery and my best friend Chi." Beau said introducing the last two.

"KC friends." KC said looking admirably at her new friends.

"KC, you are very naughty." Kipsie said, now looking disapprovingly at her little sister. "I have been so worried."

"KC sorry." KC said looking down in shame.

"Ollibee here has been helping me look for you all night." Kipsie said pointing at the little elf that was stood next to her.

"Hi!" Ollibee said nervously stepping forward to let himself be known. He was a funny looking little thing, slightly bigger than Kipsie, with pointed ears, bright yellow eyes, a little red nose and scruffy brown hair.

"No harm done." Bertie said softly after everyone had said a quick hello to Ollibee. "She's safe and sound now."

"Thanks again to you all for looking after her." Kipsie said smiling at the group of friends.

"Look everyone!" Veli gasped. "We've made it to the lake."

Everyone looked at the magnificent silver lake stretched out before them. Over the other side, stood an enormous pink snow-capped mountain.

"Let's stop and eat before we go across." Bertie suggested. "Would you care to join us Kipsie and you Ollibee."

"That would be nice. Thank you." They both replied.

Everyone sat down by the waters edge and made themselves comfortable.

"What we gonna eat now?" Geb asked. "I'm starving, we skipped lunch."

"Leave it to me." Doris said as she jumped up and dived into the water.

"What's the mad thing doing now?" Veli grumbled.

Everyone sat eyes fixed on the water waiting for Doris to re-emerge.

"Is she ok?" Chloe asked after a while. "She's been down there an awful long time."

"Of course she's ok. She is a water nymph remember." Veli replied, though he nervously looked closer at the water as if he was not sure himself.

"Are you sure she's ok?" Chloe asked again after a few more minutes had passed.

Veli knelt down and moved even closer to the water. He squinted his eyes to see if he could focus beneath the water.

"Do you see anything?" Geb asked.

"Not yet!" Veli replied. "Silly squid lips, don't know why I even care."

"Because you love me!" Doris said bursting up from the water and planting a kiss right on Veli's lips.

"Yuk! Get off!" Veli spat and wiped his lips.

"Dinner is served." Doris said as she threw a huge pile of fish on the ground and climbed out of the lake.

"I knew I'd get that kiss sooner or later." She laughed at Veli who was still spitting and wiping his lips.

"You're disgusting." Veli grumbled.

"He liked it really." Doris chuckled.

"How are we going to cook the fish?" Bertie asked.

Everyone sat and thought for a moment, and then Jordan spotted something hanging from one of Penny's branches that slightly resembled a frying pan.

"Penny, can I have that please?" He asked pointing at the pan like object.

"Of course you can." Penny replied as she took the object down from the branch and handed it to Jordan.

"Great! Now Veli, can you make a fire for us please?" Jordan requested.

Veli set about making a fire as Jordan carried on thinking about other items he could use.

"Geb, empty your coat please?" Jordan continued. "There might be something we can use in there."

"Oh you want my junk now." Geb grumbled as he started emptying his overloaded coat.

"Just get on with it Geb." Veli sighed.

Jordan hunted through the huge pile of junk that Geb had now emptied from his coat. He managed to find objects that resembled plates, cutlery and other utensils. Jordan then set about cooking the fish for everyone to eat. While he did everyone else told kipsie and Ollibee about the journey KC had been on so far and of the quest Beau had been sent on.

"So you haven't heard of "The jewel of Dahleigh" either?" Avery said as he tucked into the meal Jordan had just made.

"No we haven't, sorry." Kipsie replied as she too ate her food.

"Wow that was amazing." Geb said after he had cleared his plate. He sat back and rubbed his full belly.

Everyone agreed with Geb and thanked Jordan as they all too

cleared their plates.

"We'd better get moving." Bertie said. "We need to get across the lake before nightfall."

Everyone looked up at the sky that was already beginning to get dark.

"But how are we going to get across?" Beau asked. "There isn't a bridge."

"Maybe I can help." Ollibee said.

They all turned to look at the little elf that they had actually forgotten was there, because he had been so quiet up until now.

"No offence little fella, but what can you do?" Geb asked.

Ollibee simply smiled and walked over to the edge of the lake. He opened his mouth wide and started screaming the most high-pitched, blood-curdling scream you have ever heard. Everyone slapped their hands over their ears. Ollibee then plunged his head into the lake.

"What on earth is he doing?" Avery asked slowly lowering his hands from his ears.

They could still hear Ollibee's muffled screams from beneath the water.

"I don't know." Jordan replied. "But all these little'ns sure know how to belt it out."

Seconds later Ollibee had stopped screaming and lifted his head out of the water.

In the middle of the silver lake a whirlpool formed. It got bigger and bigger before two merpeople leapt from the centre of it and dived back into the water where the whirlpool had now disappeared.

"That's my mum and dad." Ollibee said, proudly looking at the merpeople. "They can help you get across."

"Your mum and dad?" Veli said looking totally confused seeing the obvious difference between the little elf and the merpeople.

"Yes it's a long story." Ollibee replied seeing the confused look on everyone's faces.

"This is my dad, Kullulu." He continued as he looked at the merman that had now swam over to the waters edge. "And this is my mum Liban."

"It's nice to meet you." They both said looking at the group of friends.

"Dad, please can you and mum help my friends get across the lake?" Ollibee asked Kullulu.

"Not a problem." Kullulu replied. "You can introduce us all on the way."

"But how will you get us all across?" Chloe asked.

Kullulu winked at Chloe and then swam off closely followed by Liban.

"Come on KC we had better go now." Kipsie said as the merpeople swam away. "We have imposed on this lot long enough now I think."

"No! KC not go!" KC shouted stubbornly.

"KC now be good, we have got to go now." Kipsie replied sternly.

"I suppose you need to get her home to your parents?" Geb grumbled trying to get rid of the pixies.

"We don't have any." Kipsie replied sadly. "It's just us; I look after KC on my own."

There was an awkward silence.

"Trust you to put your foot in it." Veli whispered to Geb.

Geb squirmed and walked away from the group.

"No! No! No!" KC yelled again. She jumped onto Bertie's' back and gripped onto his fur tight. "KC stay with friends."

"You're welcome to stay with us." Beau said. "We don't mind."

Geb grunted his disapproval but dare not say anything.

"Hop aboard." Bertie said. "KC has already made herself comfy."

"If you're sure?" Kipsie said as she joined her sister on Bertie's back. "I don't think KC's going to leave without a fight anyway."

Across the lake Kullulu and Liban were Gathering giant lily pads.

"I'll go and help them." Doris said as she dived in the lake and swam over to the merpeople.

"On you get!" Kullulu said as he dragged one of the giant lily pads over to the waters edge. Everyone looked hesitantly at them.

"It's ok. They are strong enough." Liban said as she swam over with her giant lily pad.

Beau, Chi and Chloe were the first to jump onto Kullulus' lily pad. Geb, Penny and Ollibee leapt onto Libans'.

"Can I get on your one Geb? Veli asked looking at the remaining lily pad that was being pushed by Doris.

"Sorry we're full." Geb laughed.

"Don't you try anything squid lips." Veli warned Doris before jumping onto the lily pad, closely followed by Avery, Jordan and Bertie with KC and Kipsie on his back.

"Right lets go." Kullulu said as he, Liban and Doris slowly started pushing the giant lily pads across the lake. As they did, everyone properly introduced themselves and told of their adventures and Beau's quest for "The Jewel of Dahleigh."

By the time they had reached the other side, night time had fallen and they were surrounded by darkness except for the silvery glow coming from the lake and the pink glow from the three moons in the sky.

"Right lets settle down here for the night." Bertie said as they all jumped off the lily pads. "It's too dark to go any further tonight."

"We'll stay here by the waters edge." Liban said. "So we can all say a proper farewell in the morning."

Veli set about making a fire and as the night before he sat and played a soothing lullaby on his guitar until everyone except him and Bertie had fallen fast asleep.

"Goodnight." Bertie said nervously getting up and walking towards a nearby rock.

"I'm uh... um... going to sleep over here." He added before disappearing behind the rock as he had the night before.

"Strange little thing." Veli said to himself before lying down and falling asleep himself.

A Mothers Love

"Wake up everyone," Chi whispered early the next morning. "Breakfast is ready."

Chi and Avery had been awake for some time before anyone else and had both gathered a pile of different fruits for breakfast, which they had laid out onto a large leaf they had found.

"Wow! Chi did you do all of this?" Beau asked as she sat up and rubbed the sleep from her eyes and looked at the feast of fruit laid out before her.

"With Avery's help." Chi replied.

Beau looked very stunned that her brother had actually helped Chi prepare breakfast.

"What, you used magic?" She asked Avery.

"Don't be silly." Chi laughed. "Yeah he flapped his wings a bit, but the only thing his hands were doing was picking the fruit."

Avery turned beet red with anger.

"Next time I won't bother!" He snapped.

"Chi stop teasing." Beau said trying to hide her own smile.
"You know he's a bit touchy about the whole magic subject."

"You can do magic?" Chloe asked as she stretched to wake up.

"Well he is suppo….." Beau started.

"Where's Bertie?" Avery interrupted. He was trying to change
the subject.

"Yes where is Bertie?" Jordan said looking around for the little
tapir.

Bertie suddenly leapt out from behind the rock he had snuck
off behind the night before. He looked as if he had been
running and was out of breath.

"I'm here, I'm here." He panted.

"Bertie, where on Dahleigh have you been?" Chi asked.

Everyone except Veli had always been asleep when Bertie had
gone off to his secret places to sleep.

"I Um... I was…." Bertie stammered.

"Them there Tapirs apparently like to go sleep in private." Veli
said, jumping to Berties' aid.

Bertie nervously looked back at the rock he had just emerged
from behind.

"So Avery, did I over hear someone say you can do magic?" He
said now trying to change the subject again. "What magic can
you do then?"

"He doesn't." Beau answered before Avery had a chance to. "He's meant to but he doesn't."

"Yeah thanks sis." Avery snarled at his sister. "You weren't meant to tell anyone."

"Oh it's no secret. Everyone knows already." Chi laughed. "Well everyone except your dad that is."

"We don't know." Geb tactlessly pointed out.

"Stop teasing him." Beau laughed. "You know HE'S a big sissy when it comes to magic."

"You know why I don't do it!" Avery shouted now turning so red with anger he looked as if he would burst at any minute.

"Look! Calm down." Bertie said. "Avery obviously doesn't want to talk about it."

"Well I might as well tell you now." Avery sulked. "Seeing as apparently everyone else seems to know already."

"Only if you want to, mate." Jordan said putting a friendly hand on Avery's shoulder.

Avery picked up a piece of fruit and took a bite, prompting everyone else to start eating. They all sat silently eating eyes fixed on Avery waiting for him to speak.

"I'm scared of it, alright!" Avery blurted out. "There, I said it. I am scared of magic."

"That's nothing to be ashamed of." Veli said. "I'm a big brave troll and even I get scared sometimes."

"Just like a green-bellied goblin." Doris chuckled.

"Look I told you Squid Lips, I am not a goblin!" Veli snapped at Doris.

"As he said, it's nothing to be ashamed of." Geb interrupted before Veli and Doris got into another of their quarrels.

"It is when you're the Prince." Avery replied. "I'm expected to do it all."

"I didn't think of that." Chloe said. "Albert did tell us about all the different coloured fairies, but he never mentioned silver ones."

"That's just it." Avery continued. "Chi for example, being blue means he has the gift of creating music. One day I am going to be King of the fairies, gold, just like my dad and that means the greatest magic of them all. Gold means you can do all the fairy magic but every time I try it goes so wrong."

"I'd say." Beau laughed. "Once he was trying to do the rain trick."

"That's where you can make it rain anywhere you want." Chi interrupted. "The sort of thing a green nature fairy would do. Just like my dad."

"Instead he made it snow in the palace continuously for a week." Beau continued. "We had to tell dad that he must be ill and the white spots he saw were part of the illness. We had to make him stay in bed all week until the spell had worn off."

"Yeah I still can't believe he fell for that one." Chi laughed.

"It's not funny." Avery said trying not to laugh himself. "Dad honestly thought he was really ill."

"Lucky mum backed you up though." Beau added.

"That makes it even worse though." Avery said seriously. "Mum's always hiding my secret from dad. He really thinks that one day I'm going to carry on his legacy and be as good a king as he is. How am I going to tell him I can't even do the simplest of spells?"

Nobody knew what to say and Avery looked sorrowfully down at the floor.

"Chin up little fella." Geb said breaking the awkward silence. "Dads can sometimes put a lot of pressure on their sons; he's your dad he will understand. I did when my s..."

"You have a son?" Avery interrupted looking suddenly up at Geb.

"Did I say my son?" Geb said quickly. "Silly me I meant my dad. When I decided to go my own way, he was ok about it. He had big plans for us but I had plans of my own you see and he didn't seem too interested in the same things as me but he understood."

"Talking of son's" Bertie said, looking toward the two merpeople. "I want to know how young Ollibee here is your son."

Kullulu and Liban were lying on the bank at the edge of the lake swishing their tails in the water. Ollibee was sat down beside them. Everyone's attention turned their way.

"Yes the difference is slightly obvious." Kullulu the merman laughed.

"It's all down to me really." Liban said. "Before I met my dear husband here I wasn't a mermaid."

"Uh!" Everyone said together now looking even more confused than before.

"I was an Oceanid." Liban continued. "A water nymph, just like you Doris. One day I met this handsome merman and fell hopelessly in love with him. The problem was Kullulu lived in the water and an Oceanid, although they can breathe under water for a very long time, they cannot live there. We were so in love we just wanted to be together all of the time, luckily the king of the merpeople saw how strong our love was and offered to help by turning me into a mermaid; obviously, I jumped at the chance."

"Aw that's so romantic." Doris said looking up at Veli and fluttering her eyelashes. "Don't you agree Veli?"

Veli huffed and turned away refusing to answer the question.

"But that still doesn't explain why Ollibee is an elf." Bertie said looking still rather puzzled.

"Well we've been told he'll stay an elf until he's a bit older." Kullulu answered. "We're not sure why though."

"And then what?" Avery asked.

"And then we don't know." Liban said frowning. "Apparently it can go either way; you see no one is really sure because merpeople up until now had always married other merpeople. Ollibee will end up either a merman, or an Oceanid or even a mixture of both."

Everyone looked totally baffled and was all staring at Ollibee as if they were trying to imagine what a half Oceanid, half merman would look like.

"So where does Ollibee live then?" Chloe asked. "He can't live in the water with you."

"Yes I must admit it did cause problems." Liban replied. "Since he was born we've had to pretty much spend most of our time at the bank of the lake, we soon adjusted though and made it work, juggling time with Ollibee and the time we needed beneath the water. We worked in shifts most of the time while Kullulu cared for and built a home at the water's edge for Ollibee, I would go to our true home beneath the water, do what was needed there, and visa versa. We make a pretty good team."

"Well I think it's utterly romantic." Penny said dreamily.

Beau, Chloe, Doris, and Kipsie instantly agreed, all baring the same gooey-eyed dreamy look as Penny.

"Sissy's!" Avery coughed under his breath.

Jordan and Veli overheard and started to chuckle.

"Well we think it is." Beau said giving Avery a disapproving look. She then turned to smile at the merpeople and their son.

"Thank you. So do we." Liban said looking adoringly at her husband and Ollibee.

"I wish our mum was happy like you two are." Chloe said sadly. "She always seems so lonely."

Beau put her arm around Chloe and gave her a comforting squeeze.

"Mum is happy." Jordan said yet with the same sad look on his face. "She has us. And she's always smiling."

"Not at night." Chloe said. "At night I hear her cry sometimes."

"I know me too." Jordan said sadly.

He knew that if he believed that his mum was happy and smiling all the time he could keep up the pretense just as much as his mum did.

"Where's your dad then?" Kullulu asked.

Both the children shrugged their shoulders.

"Not sure. We don't see him anymore." Chloe replied.

"More like he couldn't even be bothered with us." Jordan huffed. "He was no good anyway."

Jordan stood up and walked away from the group as if he wanted to avoid the subject. He stood to the side with his back to the group, his head held low as he scuffed at the floor with his foot. Everyone could see that this subject was obviously very painful.

"Why don't you see him anymore?" Geb said tactlessly, not seeing that the subject should have been dropped at this point.

"Geb!" Veli whispered trying to shut him up.

"It's ok." Jordan said still scuffing at the floor. "Our dad wasn't very nice at all; he always shouted at our mum, I used to hear him at night when I was in bed shouting really nasty things at her making her cry. Chloe was still a baby when he left and now he doesn't even bother with us at all."

Everyone just sat in silence for a while as nobody really knew what to say.

"So now your mum's on her own?" Geb asked, again tactlessly not realising when to be quiet.

"Geb!" Everyone now said trying to make Geb realise that now was not the time to push the subject.

"What!" Geb said, clueless as to why everyone was having a go at him.

"Honestly it's ok." Chloe said smiling sweetly at Geb. "Yes mum is all on her own, but she says she doesn't need anyone else and that we are all she cares about, but I think really she'd like to live happily ever after just like in her stories."

"She tells you stories?" Chi asked.

"Yes. She is wonderful at making them up." Chloe replied. "She even draws us pictures about her stories, they're great!"

"She sounds very special." Chi said now also looking very sad. He had never known his mum as she had died when he was only a baby.

Beau looked pitifully at her best friend, she knew what he was thinking yet she didn't say anything she just put her hand on Chi's and smiled knowingly at him.

"She is very special." Jordan said now rejoining the group. He totally adored his mum, as did Chloe. "She does so much for us and all her friends. Sure, she's had some bad times but she never shows it. She always smiles and does everything to make sure that we're happy. We don't need a dad, we have her."

"So how are we going to conquer this mountain?" Bertie asked swiftly changing the subject before Geb had a chance to ask any more uncomfortable questions. He could see Jordan had, had enough of talking about it.

Everyone looked up at the magnificent pink snow-capped mountain.

"It'll take us days to go over that or even around it." Veli said looking daunted by this prospect.

"We know a way." Kullulu said. "Half way up the mountain is a tunnel that goes right through the centre of the mountain to the other side."

"We used to meet at the river on the other side when I was still an Oceanid," Liban said."

"No. We used to race each other to the other side." Kullulu corrected laughing, and then looked lovingly at Liban. "Liban would race through the mountain and I'd take one of the rivers."

Everyone was now looking around the base of the mountain where they could see two very narrow rivers branching from the silver lake around either side of the mountain.

"Why can't we go that way then?" Veli asked.

"The lily pads are too big to go down the rivers." Liban replied.

"Well what are we waiting for?" Kipsie said jumping onto

Berties back. "We'll race you to the other side."

This was obviously a challenge to the merpeople.

"You're on." Kullulu accepted. "Ollibee you stick close to them make sure they don't cheat."

Kullulu winked at his son and ruffled his hair before diving into the water and swimming towards one of the rivers. Liban promptly followed. No one else moved for a while and then suddenly they all jumped up at once and raced towards the mountain. Bertie waited while KC jumped on his back to join her sister.

"Gee up Bertie." KC said gripping a bit of Berties fur and kicking her heels as if she were riding a pony.

Bertie rolled his eyes and rushed to catch up with everyone else who was already making their way up the mountain.

"I'm getting to old for this!" He puffed.

<u>The Darkness</u>

It didn't take them long to race up the path leading up the mountain and as Kullulu had said, there was a huge opening that was obviously the tunnel that led through to the other side. When they got to it, they stopped to rest and wait for Bertie who was still trailing behind.

"Come on little fella, nearly there." Veli laughed, geeing Bertie up the final stretch of the mountain.

"The added weight doesn't help." Bertie puffed, referring to the two little pixies sat on his back.

Bertie collapsed on the floor and looked completely exhausted.

"Wow!" Chloe said now standing on the edge of the ledge they had stopped at and looking out at the breathtaking view before her. They were high enough to see right back to the palace, which was now just a dot on the horizon, the colourful forest now looked like fluffy multi-coloured cotton wool balls in the distance and there was a romantic glow coming from the lake beneath them.

"It looks just like one of mums paintings." Jordan said now standing at his sisters' side and looking in awe at the view.

Everyone was now sitting on the edge of the ledge and looking out at the scenery.

"Mum would have loved it here." Jordan continued, sighing. "I bet nothing bad would happen to her here."

"Yeah I bet nothing bad ever happens here." Chloe added.

"Oh yes it does." Everyone except Bertie, Avery, Chi and Beau all said in unison to the children.

"Well we've not seen anything bad since we've been here." Chloe said now focusing her attention on the group.

"Things in Dahleigh are peaceful most of the time." Penny said still looking out at the view. "But that doesn't mean the bad isn't out there somewhere."

Penny bowed her head and looked rather sad.

"Are you ok my dear?" Geb asked.

Penny nodded her head making all the junk on her branches jingle. She then straightened her back and put on a false smile.

"I'm fine!" She said in a loud exaggerated voice. "Honest. I'm just being silly."

Nobody dare ask Penny why she had looked so sad; she obviously did not want to talk about it, whatever it was. Instead, they all turned back to the breathtaking view.

"Uh hum!" Ollibee coughed. "You do remember this is meant to be a race!"

Everyone jumped up, suddenly remembering they were indeed meant to be racing Kullulu and Liban to the other side. They all scuffled and shoved each other to be the first into the tunnel. Bertie picked himself up and hobbled after them.

"Here we go again," He sighed.

Kipsie gave him a gentle pat on the back to give him a bit of encouragement.

Inside the tunnel, it was getting dark as the group ran on in a bid to beat the merpeople to the other side. Penny the Nutty tree was so big that most of her branches were now blocking what little light was left coming from back at the entrance.

"It's so dark." Chloe said nervously, now slowing her pace from running to a slow cautious shuffle.

"KC not like dark." KC said gripping hold of Kipsie and Bertie for dear life.

"We need some kind of light." Jordan said.

"But we don't have anything." Geb said as he searched his coat hoping to find something.

It was now so dark that everyone had stopped.

"Well we need to think of something." Veli said bumping into something. "I can't see a thing."

"Ello handsome." Doris said. "Throwing yourself at me now, after another kiss is you?"

She had obviously been the thing that Veli had bumped into.

"In your dreams squid lips." Veli snapped.

"I know a way of getting light." Beau interrupted.

"Sis please don't!" Avery said as if he knew what she were about to say.

"You've got to do it sometime." Beau replied. "Avery can use his magic."

"No I can't!" Avery snapped at Beau.

"Why don't you try?" Jordan said. "You never know it might work. We've got to do something I can't see a thing and seeing as you are the only one here that in theory can give us light it's got to be worth a shot ay? Besides my friend I believe you can do it if you really try."

Avery had grown very fond of Jordan, along the way they had become very good friends, so found it hard to say no.

"Oh go on then." He sighed. "I'll try. But if it doesn't work I don't want anyone laughing at me ok!"

Avery rolled up his sleeves and thought for a while. He then nervously lifted his arms and started muttering something that no one could understand, and then he started to wave his arms around. A huge flash of light shot from his fingers and then it started to rain softly right there inside the cave. Darkness fell again.

"Well he's finally mastered that rain spell." Chi chuckled.

"Stop it Chi!" Beau said trying not to laugh herself. "Please try again or we'll have to go back."

"Forget it!" Avery snapped. "I just can't do it."

"Please, it's so dark." Chloe pleaded. "And now we're getting soaked."

"ok ok." Avery sighed. "But if Chi teases me I'll..."

"Just try!" Beau interrupted impatiently.

Avery once again lifted his arms and started muttering and waving his arms around above his head.

A huge rumbling sound echoed down the tunnel and made it shake.

"Don't tell me, that's the thunder spell." Chi teased and burst out laughing.

"But that wasn't me." Avery replied. "I haven't even finished the spell."

Chi instantly stopped laughing.

"If it wasn't you..." he said nervously. "Then what was it?"

The rumbling sound came again this time a little louder than before and again it shook the tunnel around them. No one dare move or even breathe.

"I'm scared!" Chloe squealed.

The rumbling sound boomed down the tunnel again this time even louder. It was so dark and everyone started to panic.

"Avery, that light would be good right now." Veli stressed.

"What's the matter? The green-bellied goblin scared is he?" Doris teased.

Another huge rumble shook the tunnel. Doris screamed and jumped into Veli's arms. For once he didn't mind as he was too petrified to even move.

Avery quickly raised his arms and tried the spell again. This time as he waved his arms, it stopped raining and you could just make out flowers that were now emerging beneath their feet and around the tunnel.

Another, more violent rumble shook the tunnel.

"Please Avery." Jordan pleaded. "I know you can do it."

"I can't!" Avery yelled. "I…"

He was interrupted by another rumble, that this time shook the tunnel so much it knocked them all off their feet.

"Please Avery!" Everyone now pleaded. They were all now totally petrified.

The rumbling sounds were now coming one after the other and the tunnel was now shaking so much that small rocks were falling from the roof and hitting everyone.

Avery jumped up and steadied himself. He took a deep breath and raised his arms and with all he could muster, he tried the spell again. A flash of light shot from his fingers and then the tunnel lit up as if someone had just lit a lantern.

"Boo!" Boomed and unfamiliar voice.

Everyone screamed and Doris snuggled in closer to Veli who

hadn't even realised she was still in his arms. Avery froze and held his breath for stood not inches in front of him was a huge giant whose body took up the whole tunnel.

"Please don't eat me!" Avery squeaked in a high-pitched petrified voice.

The giant started to laugh. He laughed so loud that the tunnel began to shake again. Everyone except Avery huddled closer together. Avery still stood frozen on the spot; his eyes shut tight too scared to move.

The giant stopped laughing and licked his lips.

"I am a bit hungry actually." He said and then started laughing again.

Avery shut his eyes even tighter, swallowed hard and waited for the giant to gobble him up whole.

"Ah I'm just messin with ya little fella." The giant laughed. "I don't really want to eat you."

Avery nervously opened his eyes and looked up at the giant.

The giant was huge and was rather peculiar looking. It appeared to have two sides. One side looked completely different to the other. His hair was black and scruffy on one side but neatly groomed on the other, one side of he's face looked quite nasty, the eye on that side was shut. The other side of his face looked kind, even the piercing blue eye, that was open, looked friendly. The giants' clothes were also different on the right to the left. Avery couldn't help but stare at the side that looked nasty and had the eye shut.

"Don't mind him." The giant said pointing a finger to that half of his body. "He's always asleep."

"Uh!" Avery said totally confused.

"Never mind." The giant replied. "I'm Gadra. Kullulu sent me in to find you; he thought you might have got lost."

The giant thrust out his huge hand for Avery to shake.

"Hi, I'm Avery." Avery said nervously shaking the tip of the giants little finger that was still huge in comparison to his tiny hand. "And these are my friends.

Veli jumped to his feet sending Doris flying and said hello, everyone else then jumped up and nervously said hello too.

Penny was the first to step forward and properly introduce herself; she had the advantage of being nearly the same size as the giant. She then went on to introduce everyone one by one. All of them except penny still looked very petrified.

"Look at you all." Gadra laughed. "Lighten up will you. I'm not going to hurt you."

Penny was now also laughing at the look on everyone's faces.

"Yeah they were a bit like that when they first met me." She laughed. All the junk on her branches began to jingle.

"May I say how stunning you look madam?" Gadra said admiring Penny.

Penny blushed and lightly shook her head so the junk would jingle again.

"Thank you." She said. "Geb helped me with some of the accessories."

"Well he certainly has an eye for beauty." Gadra replied. "And that red lipstick looks magnificent on you."

"Why thank you Gadra. It's by trior." She replied blushing again. "I'm glad you like it."

"I'd better get you back to Kullulu and Liban." Gadra said still smiling at Penny before he turned around to lead the way. As he took a step forward, the tunnel began to shake again causing Beau to let out a loud scream.

"Oops. Sorry." Gadra said. "Think I better go a bit lighter on the old feet."

He then bent his body over and slowly lifted his long skinny leg and started to tiptoe. Everyone thought he looked quite funny and started to laugh before following the giant out of the tunnel.

"How do you know my parents?" Ollibee asked as they emerged out of the other end of the tunnel.

"Ah yes. You're Ollibee, their little son." Gadra replied smiling at Ollibee. "I knew them years ago before your mum became a mermaid. I used to help her through the tunnel when she was off to meet your dad. I tell you it was a right shock to see them again after all this time."

"What kept you?" Kullulu shouted up from the river at the base of the mountain.

"Slight technical glitch!" Beau shouted back as she threw Avery a funny look.

"There's a point." Bertie said. "Avery do you realise, you did magic."

"Yes I did. Didn't I?" Avery said suddenly realising that he had indeed mastered a spell. He puffed out his chest and looked rather proud of himself.

"Bet he couldn't do it again." Chi teased. "Let's face it he was useless back there for a while."

Avery quickly raised his arms, muttered something and thrust his arms out towards Chi. A flash of light shot from Avery's fingers and hit Chi knocking him to the floor. Flowers started popping out all over Chi's body.

"Bet I can!" Avery said in an angry yet very matter of fact way.

"That was a bit risky." Chi whined. "What if it had gone wrong? You could have really hurt me!"

"Who's to say that I didn't get it wrong?" Avery snarled.

"He has a point." Beau pointed out. "That was really dangerous."

Chi stood up and stomped down the remainder of the mountain and joined Kullulu and Liban. As he did, he picked the flowers from his body.

"Well he shouldn't have teased me." Avery sulked, although he had just realised what he had done was in fact very dangerous.

"But well done for getting two spells right in a row." Geb said tactlessly as they too approached Kullulu and Liban.

"Found them safe and sound." Gadra said presenting the group to the merpeople.

"Thanks Gadra." Liban said smiling sweetly up at the giant.

"So I take it you've met everyone." Kullulu said smiling at the group of friends.

"Yes." Gadra laughed. "Gave em a bit of a fright at first though."

Everyone nodded and also started laughing. Ollibee walked over and gave his parents a hug.

Gadra said looking down at the little elf and his parents. "He's a sweet little thing; I'm so pleased for you both. I had wondered why I hadn't seen you for such a long time; I suppose it got harder getting out once this little nipper came along."

"Yes just a bit," Both Kullulu and Liban said in unison, both looking at their son with sheer admiration.

"Sorry to interrupt, but we had better press on." Bertie interrupted. "We lost a bit of time in that tunnel and we only have a few hours of sunlight left now."

"He's right." Veli said. "Which way do we need to go now Beau?"

"Shiranne said that we have to go across a field to get to a maze." Beau replied.

"Where ya all off to then?" Gadra asked with a quizzical look on his face.

"Well little Beau here is trying to find The Jewel of Dahleigh."

Penny replied. "And as for the rest of us... well we just all kind of tagged along really."

"Why are you trying to find this jewel then Beau?" Gadra asked as he hunched himself over to look down at the little fairy.

"Well in case you hadn't noticed I don't quite look like your average fairy at the moment." Beau replied as she looked down at her grey transparent body and flapped her tiny little wings. "I've been sent on a quest so I can earn my colours and my wings; I have to go and find "The Jewel of Dahleigh.""

"Have you heard of it?" Chi added.

"No I haven't sorry but I do know someone that might just be able to help you." Gadra replied. "T'Sang-Loubes."

"Who?" Beau asked.

"T'Sang-Loubes." Gadra repeated. "She's a dragon and guardian of Dahleighs treasures."

"Then she's sure to know about "The Jewel of Dahleigh!" Beau chanted as she danced around with excitement. "At last someone that might be able to help us."

"And she lives near a maze funny enough." Gadra added.

"Is she a nice dragon though?" Beau asked nervously. "I've always thought that dragons are nasty creatures."

"Oh not at all Beau, she's very nice." Gadra laughed.

"So how do we find this T'Sang-Loubes?" Bertie asked.

"Just follow the river." Gadra replied pointing down a river that ran straight through a field just in front of them. "I can take you if you like."

"Thank you, that's very kind of you." Beau replied smiling up at the giant that towered so high above her.

"Well come on then. Let's go!" Gadra boomed as he walked off towards the river that led through the field. Everyone followed close behind him and Kullulu and Liban swam along the river beside them all. All of them seemed in high spirits as they walked along chatting to one another and telling Gadra more about Beau's quest that they all felt they were at last one step closer to fulfilling.

The guardian of treasure

"So what's T'Sang-Loubes like then?" Penny asked Gadra as they walked along the riverbank.

"Oh she's lovely." Gadra replied. "She loves to sing. In fact she sings nearly all of the time, I bet she even sings in her sleep."

Penny laughed

"Gadra, can I ask you something?" She asked nervously.

"Ask away." Gadra replied.

"Why do you have two sides?" Penny asked shyly, she hoped this question did not offend Gadra.

"Oh him." Gadra laughed referring to the scruffy side of his body. "He's my twin, apparently things went a bit wrong when I or should I say we were born, my mum said it was some kind of spell or something but she died before she had a chance to tell me anymore."

"Oh I am sorry." Penny said gently patting Gadra's arm with one of her lower branches.

"It's ok it was a long time ago." Gadra replied blushing slightly at Penny's touch. "My dad did tell me once before he passed away that my twin here was very nasty and they just couldn't cope with him so my mum got her hands on a sleeping potion that would work on him but not on me and he's been asleep ever since, unfortunately my mum died shortly after. I do have vague memories of when he was awake and from what I can remember he wasn't nice at all. This all must sound very strange to you."

"No it's fascinating." Penny said intrigued.

"Talking of fascinating." Gadra laughed and turned to look Penny in the eye. "How come you don't see many talking tree's around here?"

Penny turned away from Gadra and looked very sad all of a sudden.

"Oh I'm sorry." Gadra said. "I didn't mean to upset you."

"It's ok." Penny said turning to see if anyone else was listening. There wasn't. "When I was a very small child my parents were killed and I had a curse put on me that turned me into a tree."

"Oh penny I am sorry to hear that." Gadra said gently patting one of Penny's lower branches. "So what were you before you was a tree, if you don't mind me asking?"

"That's the thing." Penny replied sadly. "I don't remember, I don't even remember my parents, it was so long ago now."

Penny turned around to check again that no one was listening.

No one was listening as they were all chatting amongst

themselves about "The Jewel of Dahleigh." Beau was trying to guess what it looked like and what might happen when she had found it. Everyone was giving their opinion and trying to guess what colour Beau might end up.

"OOO Talking of colours," Beau said clapping her hands together. I haven't even seen yours in action Chi."

"Oh my days you haven't have you?" Chi replied enthusiastically. "Watch this!"

He held out his right hand flat and with his left hand start swirling his finger over his palm as he did blue fairy dust came out of his finger to form a small flute in the palm of his hand. He placed the flute to his lips and started playing a little tune.

"Wow!" Beau said, looking amazed at what Chi had just done

"That's not all." Chi replied, holding out the flute in his palm again he swirled his other finger over the flute, which then turned into a violin. He then tucked it under his chin and started playing a dreamy tune. "I can make any instrument I want."

Meanwhile Geb was busy trying to sell some junk from his coat to Kullulu and Liban.

"No thanks." Liban said politely as Geb thrust a twisted silver object in her face. "Maybe another time."

Geb shrugged his shoulders and strolled casually over to Gadra and Penny.

"Can I interest you in anything sir." Geb said thrusting his coat open and looking up at Gadra who even towered above him.

"Mmm let me see." Gadra said studying the items in Geb's coat. "I don't think so."

"How about something from here?" Penny asked shaking her head so all the junk on her branches clashed together. "We're business partners aren't we Geb?"

"Yes we are." Geb said smiling at Penny. "We have big plans you know."

"And ruin such a beautiful display." Gadra said looking admirably at Penny. "No I couldn't."

"Aww you're so sweet." Penny said blushing.

"I tell you what." Gadra said turning back to face Geb. "I'll take that silver thing I saw in your coat."

Geb opened his coat again. There must have been a hundred silver objects hanging inside it so Geb just grabbed the nearest one.

"This one?" He asked handing Gadra the object.

"Yes that's the one." Gadra said not even looking at the object Geb had just handed to him. He turned and winked at Penny, she knew he had just taken it to please Geb and smiled sweetly as if to say thank you.

"What's that over there?" Veli interrupted everyone and pointed across the field.

Everyone stopped talking and looked over to where Veli was pointing. Just across the field, they could see a smallish creature crawling around on its hands and knees looking for something on the ground.

"What you looking for?" Chi said walking away from the group and confidently approaching the creature.

"Oh my life! You frightened the bones out of me." The creature shrieked as he jumped up and looked very startled.

"You're a leprechaun." Chloe said who had now also left the group and joined Chi.

"Yes I am." The leprechaun said removing his hat and bowing to the two girls. "Craggles is the name."

"It's nice to meet you Craggles." Chi said bowing to the leprechaun. "I'm Chi and this is Chloe."

The leprechaun replaced his hat on his head and smiled.

"So what was it you were looking for?" Chi repeated. "Can we help you find it?"

"I was looking for a three leaf clover." Craggles replied.

"Don't you mean a four leaf clover?" Chloe corrected.

"No I meant what I said, a three leaf clover." Craggles said smiling cheekily at them.

"Are you sure?" Chloe asked frowning at the leprechaun.

"Well I'm a little unlucky you see; only a three leaf clover works for me." Craggles sang and danced around on the spot.

"But three leaf clovers grow everywhere." Chloe stated. "Isn't it the four leaf ones that are hard to find."

"Oh no not here in Dahleigh, it's the three leaf ones that are hard to see." Craggles sang again dancing around on the spot.

Chloe and Chi both looked down and studied the ground beneath them. They hadn't noticed before but the field they were walking across was actually a field of four leaf clovers.

"Wow!" Chloe cooed. "My mum could do with one of these."

Chloe knelt down, picked a four - leaf clover, and placed it carefully in the back pocket of her jeans.

"Come and meet our friends." Chi said pointing to the group that were still standing on the riverbank.

"This is Craggles." He said as he led the leprechaun to her friends. "And Craggles, these are my friends, Princess Beau, Prince Avery, Jordan, Geb, Veli, KC, Kipsie, Kullulu, Liban, Ollibee, Doris, Penny and Gadra."

She stopped to take a breath as saying all those names took it all out of her.

"Oh and that there is Bertie." She added.

"You!" Bertie said snarling at Craggles.

"Thought you'd seen the last of me didn't you." Craggles said jumping behind Chloe to hide.

"You know each other?" Jordan said looking very surprised.

"Yes we do." Bertie said grumpily.

"Yeah, thought you'd chased me off didn't you." Craggles said dancing about on the spot again.

"You're the leprechaun that was at The Estate!" Jordan said remembering the story Albert had told them in the forest back in their world. "But I thought it was Lord Holmes and Albert who chased you off."

"Yes they did!" Bertie butted in before Craggles had a chance to speak. "Don't listen to him he can't be trusted."

"Ah! Lord Holmes." Craggles said with a cheeky grin. "How is the old fella?"

"Better since you've been gone!" Bertie snapped.

"So how did you end up here in Dahleigh?" Jordan asked trying to ease the growing tension between Bertie and Craggles.

"THEY! Chased me into the house." Craggles replied, emphasising the word they. "I ran into one of the rooms and tripped on something, the next thing I knew I was here."

"You must have fallen into the painting." Jordan said.

"Mmm yes I do remember a big painting." Craggles said. "Anyway I've been here ever since."

"Best place for you." Bertie grumbled. "Lord Holmes's gardens have never looked so good."

"That's why you were ripping up his garden." Chloe said remembering what Albert had told her about the leprechaun. "You were taking all his three leaf clovers."

Craggles didn't reply he just gave Chloe a very cheeky grin and nodded his head.

"You must have had lots of luck then." Chi added.

"Yes I did!" Craggles said enthusiastically. "It was full of them.

Not like here in Dahleigh."

"Hold on a minute!" Chloe said remembering what else Albert had told her about the leprechaun. "So why did you kill his animals?"

Everyone took a step back from Craggles and looked totally horrified.

"And to think I was being so nice to you." Chi snapped. "You nasty little thing!"

"I don't know what you are talking about." Craggles said nervously. "That wasn't me; I loved Lord Holmes's animals. I would never..."

Craggles was so upset he couldn't finish the sentence. He put his head in his hands and started to cry.

"Oh stop it you know you did do it!" Bertie snapped impatiently at the leprechaun. "Lord Holmes saw you."

"I promise it wasn't me." Craggles said still sobbing.

"Well if it wasn't you. Who was it?" Chloe said she wasn't sure whether to believe Craggles or not.

"It was him!" Bertie snapped again. "Lord Holmes saw him, I told you."

"It wasn't me." Craggles protested his innocence again. "I bet it was Kalki."

"Who's Kalki?"

"He's a shape shifter." Craggles replied. "He's not very nice at all, he's dark and evil. I'm scared of Kalki and try to stay out of his way."

"I've heard of shape shifters." Veli said. "Aren't they the creatures that can change their appearance to look like anything they choose?"

"Yes that's them." Craggles said. "And they are all evil."

"Not all of them." Bertie snapped. "Some of them are nice."

"Oh and you know many shape shifters do you?" Craggles mocked.

"Well um... no, but well...anyway who's to say that you're not that shape shifter trying to trick us." Bertie stammered.

"No! Not me." Craggles said softly. "I'm a good leprechaun I promise."

Craggles looked at the group with eyes that pleaded with them to believe him.

"Ok we believe you." Chloe said smiling at Craggles. "Don't we Bertie?"

Bertie refused to answer; he just grunted and cautiously nodded. He obviously didn't trust the leprechaun at all.

"So Bertie my old pal what brings you to Dahleigh?" Craggles said trying to break the tension between them.

"I'm here to keep an eye on Jordan and Chloe." Bertie replied. "And I'm not your pal!"

"There's no need to be like that." Craggles sulked and turned to face Jordan and Chloe. "So why are you here then?"

Jordan told Craggles about the competition and being sucked into the painting. He then told of how they had been sent to help Beau on her quest for "The Jewel of Dahleigh."

"You should come with us." Chi said once Jordan had explained everything. "We can help you look for three leaf clovers on the way."

"Can I? Can I really?" Craggles said looking totally astonished that he had been invited to go along with them.

"Yes really." Beau laughed. "It's not as if we haven't already picked up a few strays along the way."

"No one ever wants me around." Craggles said. "It's because I'm so unlucky you see."

"I'm sure you're not really." Chi replied. "It would be nice if you came along."

Craggles was so excited he leapt forward to give Chi a hug but as he did his little legs got tangled and he fell flat on his face.

"See what I mean." He said as he picked himself up off the floor and turned bright red with embarrassment.

"Craggles funny!" KC said laughing so much she was clutching her stomach and rolling around on Berties back.

"KC don't laugh." Kipsie snapped.

"It's ok." Craggles laughed. "I'm used to it."

"Are you sure you want to trust him?" Bertie whispered to

Avery so nobody else could hear. "How can you be sure he's telling the truth?"

"Well I'm sure he is." Avery whispered back. "And if he stays with us we can keep a close eye on him just in case he isn't."

Bertie smiled coyly at Avery and then gave him a knowing wink that told him it was a clever idea.

"Come on gang, we'd better get a move on." Gadra said. "We can't hang around here all day."

Gadra, Penny, Bertie and Geb started to walk off along the riverbank again, closely followed by everyone else who were now all listening to funny stories Craggles was telling about the mischief he got up to at The Estate.

"We're here." Gadra said after they had had walked for at least another fifteen minutes and reached the end of the field.

Just up ahead was a cave.

"T'Sang-Loubes are you there?" Gadra called as they approached the cave.

A shuffling noise came from inside the cave.

"T'Sang-Loubes, I know you're there." Gadra called again. "It's me, Gadra."

Just then, a pink dragon emerged from the cave with a huge grin on its face.

"Gadra my friend, how have you been, come give me a hug and one of those huge cheesy grins." The dragon sang as it bounded over to Gadra.

"Ah T'Sang-Loubes my dearest friend, it's good to see you."
Gadra said as he gave the dragon a huge hug. "I'd like you to
meet my friends."

Gadra introduced everyone and started to explain of how they
were all helping Beau search for the "The Jewel of Dahleigh"

"So that's when I thought of you." Gadra said once he had
finished explaining the rest. "I thought you might have heard of
this Jewel that they are trying to find."

"So do you think you can help us T'Sang-Loubes?" Avery
added.

"I'll have to think for a while, but I hope I can help you's, oh and
please by the way, you may just call me Loubes." The dragon
sang.

"While you're having a think, I'll rustle us up something to eat."
Gadra said walking off towards the cave. "Is that ok Loubes?"

"Not a problem, you know where everything is." Loubes sang
back.

Gadra nodded at the pink dragon and disappeared into the
cave.

"He can cook?" Penny said sounding quite impressed.

"Boy can he cook." Loubes replied this time in her normal
voice. "Just you wait this is going to be the best meal you have
ever eaten."

Everyone settled themselves down next to the river next to
Kullulu and Liban and told Loubes more about their journey so
far.

"Grubs up." Gadra said emerging from the cave some time later with a huge pot in his hands. "Hope you all like vegetable soup."

He put the pot down and went back into the cave to fetch a pile of bowls that looked like they had been made from hollowed out rocks. He then served everyone a bowl of soup.

"You're right Loubes that was the best meal I've ever eaten." Jordan said as he cleared his bowl. "And I never eat my veg at home."

"Yeah you wait till I tell mum." Chloe laughed.

Everyone praised Gadra for his cooking as they too all cleared their bowls.

"Thank you." Gadra replied. "So Loubes have you heard of this jewel or what?"

"Well you said something about a maze." Loubes began. "I do know that there is a very sacred Jewel at the centre of the maze over there, but I don't know what it's called, what it does or even what it looks like, it's the only jewel in Dahleigh that I don't have to guard."

Everyone was now looking towards a long hedge that Loubes had pointed at.

"That must be it!" Beau chanted excitingly.

"I've always wondered what it was that was in that maze." Loubes sang. "If only you knew how frustrating it can be, not knowing about the only jewel I can't see."

"Come with us then." Beau said. "I know I'd want to know if it was the only jewel I wasn't allowed to guard."

"Do you know your way through the maze?" Bertie asked very politely.

"No, I'm sorry I haven't a clue, but I know there's an entrance there we can go through." Loubes sang as she pointed to an opening in the hedge that ran along the whole end of the field right up to T'Sang-Loubes cave.

"Jordan is really good at mazes." Chloe chimed; she liked the way Loubes sang every word. "He plays maze games on the computer all the time at home."

"Then Jordan should lead the way." Beau said.

"We'll have to stay here." Kullulu said. "The river ends here."

"Oh what a shame." Chi said. "If only you could come with us."

"Take Ollibee with you and we'll hang around here and wait." Liban suggested. "He can give us a call on your way back."

"Ok then." Beau replied smiling down at the merpeople and then turning to face everyone else. "Let's go everyone."

They all said their goodbyes to Kullulu and Liban and followed Jordan and Avery who were now walking towards the entrance of the maze.

"Good Luck!" Kullulu and Liban shouted after them as they all disappeared into a gap in the hedge.

The Jewel

"This is so exciting!" Loubes sang as they walked down the first narrow path of the maze.

"You have a lovely voice." Chloe said smiling up at Loubes. "I love singing and dancing."

"Why thank you my dear, so nice of you to say, lets make up a song and dance on the way." Loubes sang cheerily.

Chloe, Loubes, Beau, Chi, Doris and Craggles all chuckled and started to sing and dance.

"Oh brother!" Jordan said rolling his eyes. "That's all we need, all of them at it!"

Avery, Bertie, Veli and Ollibee laughed. Penny, Gadra and Geb were not listening as they were chatting amongst themselves and scouring the floor for more objects to sell or hang from Penny's branches.

"Look at us all." Avery laughed. "If only my dad could see us now, he'd have loved this."

"Bit of an adventurer then?" Bertie asked.

"Well kind of he just likes talking and helping others, he would have loved you lot." Avery replied. "He always talks about the adventures he had and creatures he'd met when he was a young prince like me. I wish I could be more like him and not too frightened to even leave the palace because I couldn't get the hang of the whole magic thing. My dad could do every spell in the book by the time he was my age"

"He sounds great." Jordan sighed.

"Oh I'm sorry mate. I was waffling on a bit there." Avery said looking as though he felt extremely guilty about going on about his dad like that. "I didn't mean to..."

"Don't be silly." Jordan laughed. "Just because I don't see my dad it doesn't mean you can't talk about yours. Don't get me wrong I do miss having a dad just not my dad. But you can talk about yours you know."

"I'm sure one day you'll have someone to call dad." Bertie said. "In fact I'll bet my life on it."

"I hope so." Jordan sighed.

"So what way should we go now?" Veli asked as they reached the end of the narrow path.

Jordan looked left down one narrow path way then right down another and scratched his head.

"This way." He said seconds later, choosing to go left.

"Please can we rest a minute?" Bertie asked after they had walked quite a long way down the second pathway. "I'm worn out."

The journey had obviously taken its toll on the poor little old tapir and he was absolutely exhausted. Everyone stopped so Bertie could rest.

"Let me lighten the load a bit little fella." Gadra said holding his hand out for Kipsie and KC to jump onto. "And while we're here we can eat."

"Penny do you mind?" He added as he gently placed Kipsie and KC onto one of Penny's branches. "They'll be safe up there."

"Of course I don't mind looking after the little darlings." Penny cooed enthusiastically. "Don't worry little ones Penny's here to look after you now."

"Pretty Penny tree." KC said looking adoringly down at Penny.

"Thank you Penny." Kipsie said. "And thank you Bertie for getting us this far."

"Not a problem." Bertie puffed still looking very worn out.

"So who's for pie?" Gadra said pulling a pie out that was hidden in one of the objects on Penny's branches.

"Wow where did that come from?" Craggles asked.

"I whipped it up back at T'Sang-Loubes cave." Gadra replied as he handed Craggles a slice. "Penny kindly let me hide it so I could surprise you with it."

"Aw thanks Gadra." Everyone said almost in unison.

Everyone sat down on the floor and tucked into a slice of fruit pie. It was the most wonderful pie they had ever eaten.

"How are you feeling now Bertie?" Chloe asked as she ate her last mouthful and tenderly stroked Bertie behind the ear.

"Much better. Thanks." Bertie replied. "In fact I'm ready to move on now."

Jordan had already got up to have a little look about to help decide what way they should go next.

"Right this way!" He called once he had chosen his route.

They all jumped up and followed Jordan as he walked down this path and that, turning left here and right there. Avery, Bertie, Geb and Ollibee all walked along side Jordan chatting, while Penny and Gadra followed behind, both cooing over Kipsie and KC. Veli was now walking with the rest of the group; he had tucked his guitar under his arm and was making up a tune to go with the song they had all made up. Chi had also summoned up a flute to play.

When Jordan and Chloe went to meet a Lord,

Little did they know, they'd be far from bored,

For he had a secret, something quite rare,

A magical world, only with them he would share,

A fantasy Painting that sucked them right in,

Now this is where their adventure begins,

They were sent to a fairy, so grey and so dull,

To earn her wings and her colour was her only goal,

Avery her brother was ordered along,

If only they knew that, his magic's all wrong,

Bertie jumped in and gave them a fright,

When he opened his mouth and the words came out right,

So off the five went on this quest set for Beau,

What lay in store for them, did anyone know?

First, they met Geb trying to flog them his junk,

Lucky Veli was there to calm the great lunk!

Now there was seven to go on with the quest,

Geb got a shock when he thought he knew best,

A snap on the finger from the sweetest pixie,

She clamped her jaws tight, that naughty KC!

The poor little thing had got lost on her way,

Beau offered to help and with them she could stay,

Now Veli had claimed that he was a brave troll,

But then Doris jumped out and over he bowled,

She batted her eye lids and wiggled her hips,

But Veli just shouted. "Get off me squid lips!"

Then what a surprise beau could not pretend,

The Jewel of Dahleigh

How happy she was to see her best friend,

Chi had just also received his colour of blue,

Sweet music is now what he can do,

Now Geb was acting as strange as could be,

When he tried to flog all his stuff to a tree,

He soon proved them wrong when it started to talk,

Penny lifted her roots up so with them she could walk,

So eleven crack on with the journey so far,

An ear-piercing sound set their backbones ajar,

How two little creatures could make such a sound?

But at least KC's sister at last they had found,

She's been searching all night with the help of an elf,

Little Ollibee there was a strange one himself,

Now who would have thought that this elf came to be?

A son of two mermaids, what a strange sight to see,

Kullulu and Liban two soul mates entwined,

Who showed them how love can make two worlds bind,

They challenged a race to new friends now made,

But then inside the tunnel their courage did fade,

Now stuck in the darkness in terror and fright,

Avery soon got the spell and gave them all light,

But he wished that he hadn't for standing quite near,

Was a two sided giant, Avery was frozen with fear,

He shut his eyes tight and said. "Oh please don't eat me!"

He squealed like a girl and shook like a sissy,

Gadra just laughed. "I won't eat you at all,"

"I've been sent here to help you all out, you fool!"

Out of the tunnel the race was now over

What a strange thing to look for a three-leaf clover,

But the unlucky leprechaun needs one today,

For his lucks not been good since they chased him away,

Now seventeen continue in the search for the gem,

Gadra remembers someone to help them,

"We'll go see T'Sang-Loubes." He said with a cheer,

"She'll know where to look and she lives quite near here,"

But the all singing Dragon was clueless to know,

About this jewel that was there to help little Beau,

Though she'd heard of a treasure, the best of its days,

A secret jewel hidden in the midst of the maze,

Now the strangest friends that you ever did see,

Entered the maze, to find "The Jewel of Dahleigh."

"I love it." Loubes sang clapping her hands together.

The whole group had now joined in with the singing and all laughed together as they continued through the maze.

"We're getting close." Beau suddenly interrupted.

"How do you know?" Bertie asked.

"I don't know." Beau replied. "I can just feel it."

Everyone stopped while Jordan studied three pathways. He looked as though he was struggling to decide what way to go and was scratching his head; every now and then he closed his eyes and quietly muttered something to himself.

"Left!" He finally said after a few moments.

As they turned left, they could see a strange white glow above a hedge in the distance.

"That's it!" Beau said with excitement. "I'm sure of it."

Everyone suddenly picked up their pace and rushed towards the glowing light that was beaming above the hedge.

"It's on the other side of this hedge." Jordan said as they reached the end of the path and faced a tall hedge right in front of them.

"Look there's an opening there!" Veli shrieked with excitement pointing to a gap in the hedge not far from where they were standing.

Jordan rushed over to the opening and then suddenly stopped and slowly turned to face Beau.

"You should go first Beau." He said. "After all, this is your quest."

Everyone stepped aside as Beau nervously walked over to the opening in the hedge. She slowly stepped through the gap, closely followed by everyone else. They were finally at the centre of the maze.

"Wow! It's amazing." Chi swooned in complete awe.

For right in the centre set on carved stone was the most precious white jewel you have ever seen, it sparkled so much that it was almost blinding.

Everyone stood with their mouths wide open it total awe of it.

"We've found it Beau." Avery jumped around with excitement and then scooped his sister off her feet and swung her around in a circle. "Sis we've really found it."

Everyone joined in with Avery's celebration dance and all hugged and kissed each other. Veli even scooped up Doris and gave her a huge kiss smack on the lips, however once he had realised what he had done he dropped her straight on the floor and spat and wiped his lips. Doris just sat on the floor for a while with the happiest, gooiest look on her face.

"So what are you waiting for?" Bertie said prompting Beau towards the jewel. "The jewel was meant for you, go on pick it up."

"Yes pick it up." Chi repeated. "This is what this whole journey was about, and then you'll get your wings and your colour."

"What now?" Beau said nervously. "You think I'll get them now."

"Well you had to find the jewel, and you have." Chi squealed with excitement. "So I don't see why not."

Beau turned and smiled sweetly at all her friends.

"I just want to thank you all so much for helping me." She said. "I couldn't have done it without you. When I first set out on this journey I would never have imagined that I was going to meet so many great friends and..."

"Oh! Just get on with it you sap!" Chi blurted out, interrupting Beau's speech, he could hardly contain his anticipation.

"Ok! Ok!" Beau said taking a deep breath. "Well here goes then."

She stepped closer to the jewel and swallowed hard. She then slowly stepped up onto the carved piece of rock beneath the jewel. Nervously she reached out her arms and took another deep breath, as she did she closed her eyes tight as if she were expecting the jewel to explode as soon as she touched it.

Everyone stood poised, for what seemed like an eternity, eyes fixed on Beau all waiting for something to happen, the anticipation was so great that nobody dare even blink.

Beau's hands hovered nervously either side of the jewel for a while and then suddenly she clasped her hands around the jewel and picked it up.

Nothing happened.

Beau just stood with her eyes shut for a moment, she had expected something amazing to happen, just as she had done when she had stepped into the rainbow at her colouring ceremony. She had expected to get her colour and wings. She slowly opened her eyes and looked down at the jewel. She then slowly looked up at her group of friends, who were still stood poised on the spot yet now they all had a look of complete confusion on their faces.

Beau knew that what she was about to say would completely confuse them even more. She looked down at the jewel once more before saying.

"This isn't it. This isn't The Jewel of Dahleigh!"

ABOUT THE AUTHOR

So Far this has been the hardest part of writing this book. So I will keep it brief and to the point. I am a mum of 3 wonderful children, wife to the most amazing Husband, daughter to the most inspirational parents and sister to two superb older brothers. I have always been interested in all things mythical and yes I do believe in fairies. I have often spent my time dressed up as a fairy for a local children's charity and that pretty much sums me up. One big fairy!

Printed in Great Britain
by Amazon.co.uk, Ltd.,
Marston Gate.